Falling for the Earl

Improper Ladies
Book Two

The ladies who misbehave and the gentlemen who love them.

MAGGI ANDERSEN

ARE YOU SIGNED UP FOR DRAGONBLADE'S BLOG?

You'll get the latest news and information on exclusive giveaways, exclusive excerpts, coming releases, sales, free books, cover reveals and more.

Check out our complete list of authors, too!

No spam, no junk. That's a promise!

Sign Up Here

www.dragonbladepublishing.com

Dearest Reader;

Thank you for your support of a small press. At Dragonblade Publishing, we strive to bring you the highest quality Historical Romance from some of the best authors in the business. Without your support, there is no 'us', so we sincerely hope you adore these stories and find some new favorite authors along the way.

Happy Reading!

CEO, Dragonblade Publishing

Pirates of Britannia Series
Seduced by the Pirate

Also from Maggi Andersen
The Marquess Meets His Match (Novella)
Beth (Novella)
White Lady Lost (Novella)

Prologue

The Pyrenees Mountains, Spain, July 1813

WEARY TO HIS bones, the boom of musket fire still ringing in his ears, although it was now eerily quiet, Captain Hugh Fairburn pulled off his gloves and his bicorn hat and entered his makeshift tent.

Arthur Wellesley, Marquess of Wellington, and the Fourth Division had achieved their objective. Marshal Soult's incursion across the border to relieve the French garrisons in Pamplona and San Sebastian had been cut off, despite the men struggling with shortness of breath in the thin air and fatigue on steep slopes as they'd marched uphill and along narrow trails, while maneuvering cannons and wagons. Fighting alongside Spanish and Portuguese soldiers, they'd been tired when they'd faced the French forces in intense combat, with musket fire, bayonets, and the artillery exchanges making their efforts difficult. But Soult's forces had eventually retreated, after failing to relieve the besieged garrisons.

Inside the tent, Hugh's batman waited. "This message just arrived, Captain Fairburn," Wickstaff said, handing the letter to Hugh.

The brief missive was from Mr. Collins, the family solicitor. Seated on the camp bed, Hugh took a deep breath, then tore it open and read it through, knowing in his heart what news it bore.

After a short illness, his father had passed, and Hugh was Earl of Dorchester.

His lordship left a letter for you, my lord, Mr. Collins had written. *He wanted you to know he had complete faith in you. He was confident he left Woodcroft in good hands and believed you would make an excellent earl. And he went to his final rest with the knowledge you will take good care of your mother and sister.*

Deeply regretful not to have been able to say goodbye to his father, Hugh shook his head, distress tightening his throat. He had planned to see his father when next in England. To make amends. But death was final. They had not parted on good terms because his father had never approved of him joining up. "It seems we are going home, Wickstaff," Hugh said, his heart heavy. "Pack the bags." He raked his hands through his dark hair and propped a booted foot on a chair for Wickstaff to rub away the dirt and mud. When he gazed into the small mirror, his blue eyes stared back at him dark with grief. "I must speak to Wellesley."

"I'm sorry to hear of your father's passing," Wellesley said when Hugh had found him in his tent and explained. "What you were able to endure and subsequently accomplish inspired the men. Of course you must sell out, but you'll be missed."

"I'm sorry to leave, sir. But I'm glad I served in the army and witnessed you and the men's triumph under such trying conditions." Hugh saluted.

Within hours, he and Wickstaff, a sturdy, unflappable York-shireman, rode toward the Channel and home, with Hugh's thoughts resting on what awaited him there. As earl, he had inherited great responsibilities: to his people, his staff, his tenants, and the House of Lords, as well as the upkeep of invested properties. Hugh would be expected to attend the king and the Royal Court. More still was his need to support those who depended on him, his delicate mother and his mutinous younger sister, plus the importance of producing an heir. He must now face the marriage his father had arranged for him many years ago, to Miss Isabel Ashton, daughter of his neighbor, Sir Phillip Ashton.

Chapter One

Bath Assembly Rooms, England, March 1814

MISS LUCY KERSHAW turned this way and that before the mirror in the ladies' withdrawing room. She bit her lips, pinched her cheeks, then smoothed her skirts, satisfied the white muslin trimmed with spring-green satin ribbons compared favorably with the other ladies' gowns here tonight. She had only completed the final hem yesterday.

Papa had insisted she come, and although she'd finally agreed to make her first appearance among Bath society, she was still concerned about the financial pressure that would place on him. He had been downhearted since his investment in an African goldmine company that had found no trace of gold. So certain of the venture's success, he'd borrowed heavily from a London cent-per-center to pay for Lucy's come out. Next week, she was to travel to London for the Season, but that looked doubtful now. She tried to hide her disappointment from her father and was determined to make the most of what Bath offered.

Lucy took a deep breath and ventured into the elegant ballroom, where the chandeliers sprinkled a myriad of sparkling lights over the dancers performing a quadrille. There were some guests here she knew from childhood, but there was always a large influx of people visiting Bath to drink the waters, bathe, and attend the functions. Tonight, the ballroom seemed to buzz with expectations as some important personages had attended. As Lucy moved through the crowd intent on finding her father, two women she knew only by name drifted past her, fanning themselves vigorously in the warm, smoky air.

"Losing money to an adventurer, I could weep," Mrs. Hoskin, a lady of middle years in a dress of violet satin, said to the lady walking beside her.

"As do I, my dear," Mrs. Vellacott, a dark-haired widow of a similar age, in gray silk, responded bitterly. "To think we accepted the advice of someone who has barely two pennies to rub together. Had I known Mr. Kershaw lacked breeding *and* financial competence, I would not have invested in the company he recommended. There was never any chance of discovering gold. I might as well have thrown my twenty pounds into the river!"

"We must warn others not to be taken in by him," Mrs. Hoskin said bitterly, her tight, fair curls bouncing.

Lucy, furious on her father's behalf, came up to them. "A broker assured my father of the company's success," she said fiercely, standing before the surprised women. "And Papa, although he gained nothing from recommending it to you, would have wanted you both to benefit from the investment." Seeing a smirk on Mrs. Vellacott's lips, Lucy propped a gloved hand on her hip and glared at the women. Upset for her father, the lie seemed to come from nowhere. "And I am surprised you don't know my father is the Marquess of Berwick's heir. I'm sure you're aware the Kershaw's are very wealthy."

Mrs. Hoskin opened and closed her mouth, seemingly struck dumb. Mrs. Vellacott, her face burning, took her friend's arm and hurried her away among the milling guests.

"Nasty women," Lucy muttered.

"Quite so," said a deep voice behind her.

Lucy spun around.

A tall, exquisitely dressed gentleman bowed before her, a

spark of humor in his startlingly light-blue eyes. "I beg your pardon. We have not been properly introduced. Dorchester. How do you do?"

Recognizing the earl by his name, Lucy sank into a curtsey. "Miss Kershaw, my lord." Mortified to have been caught out in such a blatant lie, Lucy gazed up into the earl's eyes that searched hers. He seemed so elegant and self-assured that she sank into her slippers. A horrible thought struck her. Was he familiar with the marquess's family?

She was furious the women would say such distressing things about Papa. If only she'd stopped to think of the repercussions of such a declaration. Papa was a second cousin once removed from Fergus Kershaw, Marquess of Berwick, but their branch of the Kershaw family was the poorer and lesser known one. As Lord Berwick had two sons, there was absolutely no possibility of her father ever inheriting the title.

Lucy dropped her startled gaze to the broad stretch of the earl's waistcoat embroidered with an intricate pattern in silver thread, the exquisitely cut cobalt-blue tailcoat and crisply tied white cravat at his strong throat, while waiting breathlessly for him to contradict her. She sagged with relief when he showed no such inclination and talked instead about the hot ballroom, and how crowded and smoky it was, and she could only murmur in agreement.

Lucy recalled that the Marquess of Berwick's estate was located near Carlisle, close to the Scottish border. She imagined the family would not often come to Bath or be rarely seen in London, so perhaps this would go no further. But she still wished she hadn't said it. On reflection, her father *had* mused about their connection to their wealthy relatives, but it was a tenuous connection.

She'd been guilty of the odd lie on occasion. Not wishing her friends to know how her father's gambling affected her, it had been necessary to pretend to her companions that she was interested in their more trivial concerns when she was actually worried about paying the staff wages. And there were the smaller lies. Such as when her friend Alice Grahame had asked her if she'd liked Alice's new bonnet, which had been positively ghastly, to which Lucy had replied, *"It's lovely."* But this brazen lie was dangerous! What if they found her out? Oh! She would never do so again!

"Have you tried to drink the waters?" the earl inquired.

While these thoughts were rapidly passing through her head, the impossibly good-looking gentleman seemed to wait patiently for some sort of reply. Despite her nerves, she screwed up her nose at recalling it. "I did once. It tasted disgusting."

The corners of his mouth quirked. "That bad? I wonder why people come from all over the British Isles to drink it."

"I suppose they believe in its healing properties," Lucy said. "I am in good health, so I don't need it."

His gaze roamed over her, making a flush rush up her neck. *Drat, being fair is a curse.* Dark-haired girls never shone like a glowing ember.

"You certainly appear to be in glowing good health."

There. She was right. Her face blazed. She felt the heat. Lucy resisted putting her gloved hand to her cheek and struggled to find something less inane to say. But it proved unnecessary, for he bowed again. She'd barely had time to respond with a low curtsey before he'd left her.

Lucy watched his tall, lean figure as he made his way through the crowd. He carried himself like a soldier, with the confidence of an earl. Guests bowed to him, while others moved back to make way for his passage. What must he have thought of her? Did he know she'd lied? The thought made her hot all over again. The Earl of Dorchester? She'd heard of him. Mellicent Gibson, while in London last year, had mentioned him in her letters. She had considered him a great catch until she'd discovered he was betrothed.

Lucy sighed. She remembered the twitch of his attractive lips. Had he found her amusing? Would he relate this story to the *ton* in London and make them laugh at her expense? Or even worse, would it amount to a scandal? She cringed at the thought. Surely, it didn't matter, as she wasn't to stay in London with her Aunt Mary and attend the Season now. Perhaps that was a blessing after such an embarrassing episode. With her quick temper and strong sense of injustice, she wasn't fit to mix among the scrupulously polite members of the *ton*. But the disappointment at having her dreams turn to dust still brought hot tears to her eyes.

She swallowed, and, firming her shoulders, went in search of her father. She found him in the games room at the faro table, concentrating on his next play, and her heart sank.

Lucy turned away and walked back toward the ballroom.

"What is it, Lucy?" Her father soon caught up with her.

"I'd like to go home now, Papa."

He smiled and took her arm. "The game is over, and it's stopped raining. Why don't we walk?"

With no gray in his blond hair and a trim physique, her father was still a handsome man at fifty. His smile could charm the birds from the trees, but despite her unfailing loyalty, she'd come to distrust it. Had he spent his last shilling at the table and couldn't afford a hackney? She couldn't ask him. He was never happier than when indulging in card play, even though it often put a strain on his finances.

As Lucy and her father walked along the street, Papa put his hand in his pocket and jiggled it. "I had a splendid night at the tables."

"Oh. Did you?"

"Yes. They were playing for high stakes." He turned to her, his brown eyes gleeful. "If we're careful and your Aunt Mary agrees to sponsor you, there's enough to send you to London for a Season."

Lucy stopped, her heart thudding. "Oh, no, Papa. I cannot leave you here alone."

"Nonsense. I have gained my second wind." He sobered, and

with a fond smile, said, "I want you to go, Lucy. It will do my poor old heart good to give you this chance."

Lucy sighed. She squeezed his arm, and they walked up the street in silence. London beckoned, but it had become a poisoned chalice. If only she could learn to control her tongue.

HUGH FAIRBURN, EARL of Dorchester, had come to Bath to visit his mother and sister, who had rented a house to enjoy society and take the waters. His sister, Sarah, twenty years old and some eight years his junior, drew him aside.

"I saw you talking to a young lady." Her serious, blue eyes met his, thirsting, no doubt, for any scrap of knowledge. "Who is she? Was she in need of our help?"

"Not at all. I merely made a comment in passing about the stuffiness of the ballroom."

She tipped her head to the side. "So, it had nothing to do with how pretty she was?"

"Nothing whatsoever," he said, raising an eyebrow.

"Beg pardon, Hugh." Sarah laughed, her fingers ordering the arrangement of her brown curls. "But Mama has expressed a concern about your betrothed. Miss Ashton emerged from the schoolroom well over a year ago but shows little eagerness to come to London."

"She is still young, Sarah. Surely, there's no rush."

"I'm sure I don't know why she isn't champing at the bit to marry you. You are a handsome fellow with excellent breeding." With a cheeky smile, she tucked an errant, dark-brown lock behind one ear. "Although it hasn't been announced, it's still the world's worst-kept secret. And I'm sure her parents are eager for the match."

Hugh raised an eyebrow. "You are comparing us both to horses?"

"Don't be silly." She scoffed. "Miss Ashton is very pretty."

"Miss Ashton *is* beautiful." *A rather cool beauty of late. Or was it only with him?* "She has written to say that she and her mother plan to spend a sennight in London very soon."

"That still seems vague to me. I am more than a little annoyed at Papa for placing you in this position with our neighbor."

"Hush. Don't speak ill of the dead. You loved Papa."

"Yes. And I miss him. But still…"

"This matter shall resolve itself in time." *With a disappointing marriage, more like.*

"I daresay." She held out her hand. "Come. I'll allow you to take me into supper."

"What about your loyal suitor, Lord Cardew?" Hugh looked around. "He is usually close by."

She grimaced. "Robert is not here tonight. His mother asked him to take her to some affair or t'other. She wants him to marry the Duke of Kendal's daughter, Lady Gwendolyn, and has hopes in that direction."

"Surely, it is up to Lord Cardew to decide? After all, he is twenty-five years old. That is no longer a boy."

"If only that were possible." She frowned. "But if he always does what his mother tells him to do, then he is not the man for me."

"Quite so."

Hugh smiled at his attractive sister. He hoped she meant it. She'd wasted far too long mooning over Lord Robert Cardew, heir to the Skelton Earldom. Sarah had dampened the hopes of many admirers, only wanting one man, it seemed. Hugh wished it were not so. He detested how Cardew kept Sarah guessing. It made her nervous and unsure of herself. He offered his arm. "Shall we console ourselves with food?"

Sarah giggled and put her hand on his arm. "I hope they serve some of those delicious crab patties."

An hour later, after seeking his host and hostess to offer the usual courtesies, Hugh escorted his mother and sister to their townhouse. Intent on an early night, he planned to set out for London after breakfast. As he removed his cravat at the mirror, thoughts of Miss Kershaw entered his mind. Unsurprising, as she was undoubtedly fetching, small and dainty with her blonde curls and guarded brown eyes, but it was more her fierce determination to defend her father from those two insufferable women that had struck him. So much so, before he knew it, he'd stopped to converse with her. Something he never did. And despite her being a young, unaccompanied lady of surely no more than twenty-one, who had never been introduced to him.

He almost wished for her sake that it was true about her father. It wasn't, of course. Hugh knew the Kershaw family, although not well. The marquess had two strapping sons, unlikely to turn up their toes in the near future, although one never knew what fate had in store for anyone. Hugh had experienced the vagaries of fate, while on the battlefield. There might well be other relatives in line for the title too whom he didn't know about. He frowned. Those two women could spread nasty gossip about Miss Kershaw and her father, and he had to admit to feeling sorry for her. Especially if she was to make her come out in London this Season.

What am I about? he asked himself as Wickstaff pulled off Hugh's boots. Miss Kershaw had told a lie. One could not forget that. Having no answer for his reaction, beyond his attraction to the spirited, pretty girl, which any male would have succumbed to, he let it go.

Miss Ashton was meant to make her debut this Season so they could at last move forward. He felt frustrated by inertia while waiting for his betrothed to be presented, declare their engagement official, and set the date for the wedding. Despite indulging in empty dalliances or retreating to the country to improve matters at his estate, he constantly fought wretched restlessness and almost wished himself back in the army, for at least there, his duties had kept him from dwelling too much on the unresolved matter of his betrothal. Like Sarah, he too was angry that his father had placed him in this position, after making the agreement with Miss Ashton's father, Sir Phillip, all those years ago. It had been the reason Hugh had signed up, against his father's wishes, not wanting to kick his heels aimlessly in London until Miss Ashton was out.

If his father still lived, Hugh might have been able to overturn it. The last time he and Miss Ashton had met, he'd feared his mother was right. There was a decided lack of attraction between them. But now, he had made the commitment to honor his father's wishes and would carry it through. Hugh assumed that Miss Ashton, whom he had last found rather subdued, would be enlivened once she was introduced to Society. Yet he couldn't help comparing his lack of response to her to the spark of desire he'd felt for the young lady he'd met tonight. *Best to leave that alone*, he thought grimly.

Hugh cursed. He had his mother, who wasn't in the best of health, and his sister, who refused to give up on Lord Cardew and find a suitable husband, to concern him, and he just wanted it all to be settled. The desire to spend a peaceful life at Woodcroft running his estate appealed to him more and more as he approached thirty. But he wanted to share that life with the right woman. Someone he could love and respect. Someone whose company he enjoyed.

Hugh dined the following evening with an old university friend, Lucas Beaufort, who seldom came to the city these days. Hugh had seen little of him since he'd returned to England. After Luke had lost his pregnant bride in a house fire, he'd managed his brother's estate, Longview Hall, while he'd been away on business. Now the Earl of Ballantine was married, Luke had restored the burned-out wing of his mansion and moved back there.

"Good to see you, Luke." Hugh greeted his dark-haired friend, who appeared to be more at ease than he'd been the last time they met, his face lightly tanned from working outdoors and his blue eyes filled with lively interest. "And looking fit."

They made their way to the table in White's dining room.

"Damian is blissfully happy with his lovely countess. They have inspired me to marry and fill my empty house with a family."

Hugh nodded. "Excellent news."

"Perhaps you can recommend a lady," Luke said, his blue eyes twinkling. "One you are prepared to part with?"

"No one suited to your needs," Hugh said as a waiter brought them wine. Then a pert, little face framed with blonde curls and furious brown eyes entered his mind, and he realized Miss Kershaw had never really left it. "The women I spend time with aren't inclined to marry. I cannot afford it to be otherwise." Miss Ashton's name hung unspoken in the air.

Luke's smile was one of commiseration. "Let this be a better year for both of us."

With a sigh, Hugh raised his glass. "I'll drink to that."

Chapter Two

Westminster, London, April 1814

L UCY HAD BEEN in London for a week, but it seemed longer with her aunt fussing around her. Nothing she did seemed to please Aunt Mary, who talked endlessly about how she'd brought out her two girls to be great successes after Lucy's deceased Uncle Peter had given them handsome dowries.

"Because of your father's straightened circumstances, your come out will prove more difficult than my daughters'. Anabel and Jane are now married to men of substance." Aunt Mary *tsked*, holding up one of Lucy's gowns for inspection in the bedchamber Lucy now occupied. "It is fortunate, perhaps, that he has remained in Bath."

Lucy firmed her lips, determined not to give in to the urge to defend him again. What good could it do? It would fall on deaf ears. Aunt Mary was her mother's sister. Their family was higher up the social scale than Papa's branch of the Kershaws, as her aunt constantly reminded her.

"I should not like you to make an unfortunate marriage, as your mother did." Aunt Mary's thin shoulders looked tight, and she sounded bitter as she hung up the gown. "Their marriage was the death of her."

"Mama died of the influenza," Lucy reminded her, turning

away to hide her outraged face.

"Your maternal grandfather was a baron's second son. If Caroline had married into a family who could take better care of her…" Aunt Mary began.

"Mama loved my father," Lucy said, her chest tight.

"Ah, love. What a curse it can be." Her aunt glanced at her. "I hope you have more sense than to throw away your future on an unsuitable man, my dear."

Lucy had had enough. She took the gown from her aunt's hands. "I have a frightful headache, Aunt Mary. I must lie down for a while."

"It is very muggy today, and that long trip here in a yellow bounder…" She shuddered. "It must have been horrendous. Your father, of course, having no carriage of his own. I'll send up some feverfew. Rest while I answer these invitations we've received. Then we must tackle your wardrobe. Fortunately, we have Anabel's and Jane's old gowns to update. Fashions change subtly with each Season. Scallops are now popular, and so is blonde lace. Roses, I think, for the ballgown. A dainty row around the hem." Her speculative gaze roamed over Lucy. "You are thinner than Anabel, and much shorter than Jane, but I don't think that will be a problem. I have a good dressmaker, and I gather you are adept with a needle and thread?"

"Yes, Aunt."

"I have some fashion magazines somewhere." She rushed to the door, then turned with her hand on the latch, appearing quite enthusiastic at the task awaiting them. "We have a busy week ahead."

Lucy lay her throbbing head on the pillow. It was good of Aunt Mary to go to so much trouble for her. She really must try to be appreciative and help wherever she could. Thankfully, she had always made her gowns and was quite good at sewing. And she wanted to find a man to love. Someone she could trust and made her feel safe. She hated to admit that life with her father was often uncertain and realized she had been constantly exhausted with worry about the future.

Cutting and sewing seams and adding embellishments to four old gowns occupied her for the following sennight. The white ballgown had just arrived and was the most beautiful gown she had ever seen, trimmed with silk roses, lace, and pink satin. She thrilled just to look at it.

At the end of a long, busy day, Lucy put aside dressing a bonnet and wrote to her father, trying to sound cheerful and hide her concerns. She prayed her come out would be a success and please both Aunt Mary and her father.

Her cousin Jane visited. Jane viewed the pale-blue sarsnet walking gown Lucy wore before the mirror while their maid, Maisie, sat at Lucy's feet and pinned up the hem. Lucy expected disapproval, but Jane, uncommonly tall with dark-brown hair and gray eyes, smiled.

"I'm called a Long Meg when my back is turned," she confessed cheerfully, removing her stylish bonnet. "That shade of blue was never my color. Made me appear pasty-faced," she whispered when her mother had left the room. "But there's no telling Mama."

"The apricot-colored traveling gown with the lovely Vandyke collar you are wearing is perfect on you," Lucy said, thinking her cousin looked quite the thing.

"Yes, that's what marriage does for one," Jane confessed. "Thank heavens, at last, I can dress the way I wish. Don't let Mama browbeat you into wearing something you hate. Anabel's gowns had layers of frills and ribbons, which made her look like an iced pudding!" She laughed. "You don't need such embellishment, Lucy. You are very pretty."

"You are nice, Jane," Lucy said. "It's lovely to meet you again."

"I am sorry we've seen you so rarely," Jane said. "My husband and I shall entertain this Season, so we shall see more of each other. You can even the numbers at dinner with one of Edward's bachelor friends. Perhaps he will take your fancy."

A hand on Jane's shoulder, Lucy stretched up to kiss Jane's cheek. But she dreaded being on display like a dowerless, poor relation dredged up from the country, to be offered up for some reluctant gentleman's consideration. She drew in a sharp breath. That was what she was, and she must accept it.

LONDON WAS AGOG with the news that Napoleon had abdicated the throne and been incarcerated on the island of Elba. At the signing of the Treaty of Paris, the Prince Regent had invited his allies, William of Orange, King Frederick William III of Prussia, Prince Metternich of Austria, Prince Leopold of Saxe-Coburg, and Tsar Alexander I of Russia and his sister, to London.

Hugh wandered into the smoky heat of the Forster's celebratory ball, decorated and festooned in red, white, and blue balloons and streamers, with many uniformed men, some of whom he knew, among the guests.

His friend, Jack Ross, Viscount Hereford, soon joined him. "You've missed all the excitement," Ross said, a smile in his eyes as he raised his champagne glass. He gestured toward the far corner where several gentlemen stood, blocking Hugh's view of the lady seated there. "A mix of fortune hunters and those prodded by hopeful parents."

"Do we have a new heiress on the scene?"

Ross nodded. "Well, word has it that this young, personable lady's father is heir to a fortune."

"Her name?"

Ross jerked his head in that direction. "Miss Kershaw's father is apparently the Marquess of Berwick's heir."

Hugh's eyebrows rose. "Miss Lucy Kershaw?"

Ross raised his heavy, pitch-black eyebrows, a startling contrast to his pale-blue eyes. "You look surprised. Has she escaped your notice? Well, I suppose a betrothed fellow hasn't a great deal of interest in other women." His lips quirked in a smile. "But I must say, she has adroitly avoided the gossip pages and arrived unannounced."

"Have you met Miss Kershaw?" Hugh asked, interrupting him.

"Lady Forester introduced us. Why?"

Hugh gripped his arm. "Please introduce me to her."

Ross walked with Hugh as he crossed the ballroom floor with a purposeful stride. "You seem in a rush," he said. "Well, dashed if you're not as intrigued as the rest of us, Dorchester."

"I'm surprised you didn't keep her to yourself," Hugh said wryly.

"You do me an injustice," Ross said with a laugh. "Debutantes do not interest me, even heiresses."

Hugh supposed they didn't. A large part of Ross's life was a mystery, but one thing Hugh knew was his preference was for willing widows and even married ladies, not sheltered innocents.

Several fellows stepped aside for them. Miss Kershaw, looking delightful in white silk and pink silk roses with rosebuds tucked into her glorious blonde locks, turned her head and saw him. Her eyes grew enormous, and twin spots of crimson painted her cheeks.

When a member of the orchestra announced a waltz, Hugh nudged Ross, who cleared his throat. "I'd like to introduce the Earl of Dorchester to you, Mrs. Grayswood." They both bowed to the sharp-eyed-eyed, older lady who sat beside Miss Kershaw and seemed to be enjoying herself rather more than her charge.

Mrs. Grayswood gasped and rose to her feet, pulling Miss Kershaw up by the arm. They curtsied. "Viscount Hereford. Lord Dorchester. May I introduce you to my niece, Miss Kershaw? Lucy hails from the country and has only recently come to London."

"Would you honor me with this dance, Miss Kershaw?" Hugh asked her, aware of the chorus of objections from the gentlemen behind him.

With a glance at her aunt, who nodded vigorously, Miss Kershaw murmured her assent and, resting her gloved hand on his arm, allowed him to lead her onto the dance floor.

Hugh tried to make sense of his emotions. He usually had a good handle on them, but they deserted him tonight. Bitter disappointment in Miss Kershaw was uppermost, followed by annoyance that she and her aunt should attempt to dupe the *ton* in this manner. But even stronger was the need to hear her explanation, with the lingering hope he wrongly accused her. Perhaps it was her aunt, a social climber if ever he saw one, who'd persuaded Miss Kershaw to be part of this ruse. No, there was no way of getting around it. It was Miss Kershaw herself who'd started the rumor in Bath, though he feared she would deny it.

The music began, and she came stiffly into his arms. Miss Kershaw was small, he discovered with surprise. She was so fiercely determined, he'd thought her a taller woman. He took her dainty gloved hand in his and tried not to admire the arrangement of her blonde curls dressed in silk roses and soft, white feathers. How could someone who looked so innocent be capable of such fraudulent behavior? And how could she hope to get away with it? Someone would surely write to the marquess and advise him about it. Moreover, why was he dancing with her when he should have given her a wide berth? Let other foolish fellows fall into her trap.

She lifted her chin, and her anxious eyes looked into his. "You must be thinking badly of me," she said in a low voice.

He hadn't expected honesty. "You are not an heiress?" he stated with less vigor than he'd previously intended.

For a moment, he thought she would pull away from him. But she merely shook her head, stirring a delightful blonde curl. "I have tried to tell everyone it isn't true. But no one will listen to me."

"Then how did they come to hear of it here in London?"

"I don't know," she said. "It might be Mrs. Vellacott. Is she here tonight?"

"Perhaps," he said noncommittally, while suspecting the aunt had had a hand in it.

"You don't believe me. I didn't expect you would," she said pragmatically. "Aunt Mary said as the gossip sheets had gotten hold of it, we should just ignore it, as it is likely to do more good than harm." She took a deep breath, giving him a delightful glimpse of her delectable, alabaster-skinned bosom. "But it *will* do harm, won't it? I want to go back to Papa in Bath. But I am not allowed to. I must stay here until I find a husband who has Aunt Mary's approval." She blinked. "And what man would want me when I explain? I can't marry anyone with a lie hanging over my head."

She must have been telling the truth. There was no way he could believe otherwise, while looking into her fawn-like brown eyes. Breathing in her sweet perfume, his hands settled closer, as if protecting her as he led her through the steps. He found himself making excuses for her. How many married with buried untruths? Both men and women, and yet some marriages seemed to prosper.

But he must keep a cool head. Miss Lucy Kershaw could lead any hardy male around by the nose if she so chose. Himself included. It was her lie and only that which had caused this scandal to erupt, he reminded himself, while attempting to harden his heart.

"And why should you believe me?" she continued bitterly. "You heard me tell that awful fib." She lifted her chin. "I must face the consequences of my actions."

"What will you do?" he asked, worried for her, despite himself.

"I shall run away. Sell my pearls and take the stage back to Bath." Tears flooded her eyes. "But Papa will be dreadfully disappointed. And so will Aunt Mary, who has done so much to bring me out, and my cousin Jane, who has been such a good friend."

"Would you like me to help you?" He wondered what her aunt would make of his interference. What the *ton* would make of it didn't bear thinking about.

She glanced up at him hopefully. "Could you? I would appreciate it. I don't care if I suffer the cut direct from the whole of the *ton*. It would be better than living this…this lie."

"I could put it about that the gossips are wrong," he said as he moved her to the beat of the music. "But you guessed correctly. Society would not take kindly to the false story and will believe it came from your family. Your aunt or your father, perhaps."

Her eyes widened. "Then please don't do it, my lord. I shall manage somehow."

The music ended, and he led her slowly from the dance floor. He acknowledged friends as he guided her through the crowd of chatting people.

"Don't go flying off back to Bath," he said as they approached her aunt. "Running away is seldom the answer to any problem."

"Thank you for the dance, Lord Dorchester." She dipped into a low curtsey, then rising, hurried over to where her aunt watched them intently from her chair.

Dear Lord, what was he thinking? He never involved himself in other people's dilemmas. Not among the wealthy *ton* in any event, as they thrived on any news of a person's misfortune. Now many of the guests watched him, trying to guess what the devil was he up to. An engaged man, he obviously could not marry Miss Kershaw, and to take her side in this would stir up an even worse scandal. Not to mention his dancing with her, which would give her story more credibility and bring even more suitors to her aunt's door. Perhaps one of them might, on learning the truth, love her for herself alone. It wouldn't be so very hard. There would be many men, surely, who would be keen to take Miss Kershaw to wife because of her beauty and appeal alone.

News of his actions tonight could reach Miss Ashton, and he supposed he should expect a letter demanding an explanation. Right at this moment, Miss Ashton seemed very far away.

It wasn't too late for Miss Kershaw. Once the gossip died down, there would be a happy ending when some gentleman came up to snuff.

Hugh wondered why that solution didn't please him. He never considered himself rash and rarely acted on impulse, so this was entirely out of character. A moment of madness, he decided, as he abandoned the ballroom for White's, where, but for some in the gaming room, sanity prevailed.

Chapter Three

"AN EXCELLENT FIRST ball, Lucy! You caught Sir Percy Hepburn's attention tonight." Aunt Mary sounded pleased as she and Lucy traveled home in the carriage after the ball. "His family is irreproachable, so one might overlook the sad loss of his fortune. I expect him to call on us tomorrow."

Lucy feared her aunt had come to believe the gossip. "Sir Percy thinks I'm an heiress, even though I told him the rumor is false. He laughed and said he approved of my modesty."

Aunt Mary sighed. "You'd do better not to speak of it, Lucy."

"But I cannot just ignore it! Not when it's so patently untrue." Despite the earl's warning, she just couldn't stand the idea of keeping up the lie.

"That's of no consequence." Her aunt patted her gray-brown hair. "An air of mystery never hurt a young woman in her first Season."

Lucy chewed her lip. "I don't find Sir Percy attractive, and I do not intend to marry him, so why allow him to continue to believe it?"

Aunt Mary pursed her lips. "Very well. I shall dissuade him from pursuing you. But such attention encourages more competition," she said in a pained voice. "It stirs up interest among marriage-minded gentlemen. Unfortunately, we cannot consider the Earl of Dorchester among your suitors, as it's said he is already spoken for. But it was advantageous for us that he singled you out from the other debutantes. Gentlemen are expected to invite a debutante to dance, but that doesn't change the fact that he specifically chose you. And other men follow the earl and value his opinion." Her eyes danced. "I could not have wished for a better start to your Season."

So that was why Dorchester had danced with her. Out of a sense of duty. Lucy felt unaccountably dispirited, although it would have been foolish to believe his motivations had been otherwise.

"In the ladies' withdrawing room, a debutante, Miss Nye, told me I should not have waltzed," Lucy said. "Not without the permission of one of the Lady Patronesses on the Almack's committee."

"The rules are relaxed at a private ball. Lady Jersey and Lady Castlereagh were not there tonight, nor did I see Countess Lieven. One doesn't refuse an earl's request to dance, Lucy. And heiresses can get away with a lot more than those gently bred."

"But I am not a..." Exhausted, Lucy gave up, the last of her energy evaporating with a long sigh. It was much later than she'd ever stayed up before, and she was tense for the whole evening, careful not to put a foot wrong. She thought longingly of her bed as their carriage swept around a corner into a street of tall townhouses and pulled up outside her aunt's.

Aunt Mary smiled at her as they alighted from the carriage. "I'm confident it will all work out perfectly. You will see." She started up the steps to where a servant waited at the open front door. "Tomorrow, we must choose the gown for you to wear to Jane's dinner party on Saturday evening. You must make a good impression. So please try to smile!"

"Yes, Aunt." Lucy followed her inside.

On Saturday evening, she sat at the long dining table opposite a friend of her husband, Edward. Although Mr. Nash's mode of dressing, with a high collar beneath his chin and an elaborately tied cravat, was not to her taste, there was really nothing to dislike about him. But when he continually smiled at her across the table, and even raised his wineglass and saluted her at Edward's call for a toast to the end of the war, she fidgeted with her napkin.

"What do you think of Mr. Nash?" Jane asked once they were alone together in the bedchamber tidying their hair while the men remained at the table to drink their port and talk about politics, horse racing, and Tattersall's auction house.

Lucy expected the men's conversation would be far more interesting than Jane's at this moment. Why were women not allowed to give voice to their opinions on important matters?

"He seems nice," Lucy said cautiously. She found him rather too young, which was probably unfair when he was several years older than her.

"Just 'nice'?" Jane's brush paused over her hair. "That's a shame. He is the best-looking of Edward's friends. And he has an income of two thousand pounds a year, I'm told, which you must agree isn't shabby."

"No. It… It sounds like a lot."

Jane laughed. "I suspect he'll call and invite you to join him on a carriage ride to the park. You'll be able to discover more about him."

The guests played spillikins and card games for the rest of the evening. During a game of whist, Mr. Nash revealed his determination to win and appeared cast down when Jane and Edward triumphed.

"It takes a lot to beat my wife at cards," Edward said, lounging back in his chair and gazing fondly at Jane. Narrow-shouldered and not what one would call handsome, the fair-haired gentleman seemed a good-natured man. Lucy liked him.

"It helps to have an excellent partner of your caliber, Edward," Mr. Nash observed. "But one rarely plays with one's spouse. It really isn't the done thing."

Edward laughed and slapped him on the back, calling him a sore loser.

But Lucy sensed Mr. Nash regarded women as inferior, and as she was his partner, the suggestion hovered in the room that she'd somehow failed him. She wasn't sure how. She thought she'd played well enough. Papa had taught her to play the game years ago.

As Jane had suggested, when the evening drew to a close, Mr. Nash invited Lucy to ride with him the next day in his carriage to Hyde Park. Tempted to refuse but unwilling to disappoint Jane, she accepted. Perhaps she'd been hasty in her opinion of Mr. Nash. He suffered in comparison to Lord Dorchester, as any man would. She urged herself to forget the earl, for hoping to see him again was foolish. And she must keep her head. She could not afford to yearn for the unattainable.

When she rose the next morning, she read *The Morning Chronicle* and *The Times* at breakfast, searching for an announcement of the earl's coming wedding, but she failed to find it.

Her aunt observed her over the table. "I hope you're not a bluestocking, niece," she said with a sigh. After Lucy had mentioned she thought Mr. Nash very young, the notion that she might prove difficult to launch hung in the air.

"Heavens, no, Aunt. I like to read about who among the *ton* is getting married. London Society is so much more exciting than one finds most of the time in Bath." She thought of partnering with old Mr. Crabbshore in a country dance when he'd clacked his teeth while they'd danced and almost shivered at the thought of going back there.

"Indeed. I am pleased you are finding it so." Slightly mollified, her aunt reached for the butter.

Mr. Nash arrived punctually at five o'clock. He assisted Lucy up onto the seat of a high-perch phaeton and settled in the maid, Maisie, whose eyes were like saucers. "My, this is a most impressive vehicle," Lucy said, as they careered around a corner. She could hear Maisie moan in fear and felt a little nervous herself as she looked down at the cobbles, which seemed a fearful distance away.

Having managed to round the corner safely, Mr. Nash stood and cracked the whip, and the horses took off at a canter along the road as she clung on. "It's up to the mark," he said, turning to her with a pleased smile.

Once again, Mr. Nash's collar sat high under his chin, with an intricately knotted cravat and a frilly shirt front. The smell of pomade wafted over to her when he slapped the reins. He wore a bright-blue coat and yellow pantaloons with highly polished top boots. A spotted yellow-and-white handkerchief fluttered from his pocket. Lucy realized she was in the presence of a pink of the *ton*. She had heard of them but had never seen one in Bath.

The carriage reached the park, and they entered the South Carriage Drive. As Mr. Nash drove along the crowded thoroughfare, a gentleman riding down Rotten Row hailed him. As Mr. Nash called out to him, Lucy watched the splendid horses dancing along and failed to notice the glossy, black landau approaching until it was almost beside them. The gentleman touched the brim of his hat. Seated beside him was a young woman and her maid. In a flowery bonnet, the woman stared with interest at Lucy. She was very beautiful with a delicate, sensitive face. Lucy's chest tightened and she fiddled with her gloves.

"My lord." Mr. Nash bowed from the waist, which proved difficult while keeping his horses in check.

"Nash." The earl nodded, whip poised to move his fine thoroughbreds on.

"The Earl of Dorchester. An army man, and a known Corinthian," Mr. Nash said, his voice taking on an important note after the earl's carriage had moved away. "I wasn't aware he knew me. But word gets around, especially since I've joined White's Club."

"What is a Corinthian?" Lucy asked, gazing after them.

"You don't know?" Mr. Nash laughed. "I see I shall have to educate you in these matters. A Corinthian is a man about Town and a fine sportsman. I've seen Dorchester box at Jackson's and fence at Angelo's Fencing academy. He's a fine shot at Manton's too."

Lucy wondered if Mr. Nash followed the earl about. "Who was his companion?" She tried to resist craning her neck as the landau drew farther away.

"Lord Dorchester's betrothed, I imagine, Miss Isabel Ashton. We've not yet met. I doubt she often comes to London."

Lord Dorchester had looked imposing in the multi-caped greatcoat and tall beaver hat. His startlingly blue eyes had rested on her for the briefest moment. He'd nodded his head to acknowledge her, before moving on. He had the bluest eyes she'd ever seen, like the waters of the Mediterranean, at least as far as she remembered from a painting.

"I suppose we will hear news of his wedding soon enough," Mr. Nash mused. "A grand affair, most likely held at St. George's. The guests will number in the hundreds. It would be good to be seen there. I wonder if it might be possible? Perhaps I know someone…" He lapsed into contemplation.

He drove Lucy home, leaving her to her own thoughts.

WITH MISS ASHTON and her maid seated beside him, Hugh guided the horses through the park gates and turned into Park Lane. It frustrated him to see Miss Kershaw riding with Nash, when he knew he was unworthy of her, though it was hardly any of his business. Hugh glanced at his betrothed's profile. She looked troubled. "You should have sent me some warning. I would have accepted a few suitable affairs, not Almack's or balls, of course, until you are out, but there are picnics and dinner parties and whatnot. London is busy with many interesting venues now the war is over."

"Mama keeps me busy calling on her friends. I suppose I am out." Her face pale beneath the bonnet, she turned to him, her hazel eyes anxious. "I wanted to see you."

"And I you." He smiled, then turned to maneuver around a cart piled high with furniture. "It's been a while, hasn't it?"

"Yes. It has," Miss Ashton said thoughtfully.

"I planned to visit. We could have gone riding. But here we are. Tell me all the news from the country."

She looked startled. "News?" Her laugh sounded strained. "What news of interest is there worth discussing from the depths of the Kentish countryside?"

He smiled sympathetically. "Little, I imagine." He studied her. "Have you been terribly bored?"

She shook her head. "I am always busy. Dining with neighbors and filling my days with attending dance lessons, French tutors, sketching, and embroidery. The only time I have to myself is when I ride, stroll in the gardens, or visit the church. I've taken to arranging the flowers, which I quite like."

"It's a difficult period waiting for your life to begin, Miss Ashton. I remember Cousin Avery complaining that life was passing her by. And now she is happily married with two children. Once you attend the Season, everything will change, will it not?"

"I shouldn't complain. I did attend an assembly dance in Canterbury. And I'm to be presented to the queen at one of her drawing rooms in July."

The prospect didn't seem to please her. He would have expected meeting the queen to excite any young woman, and that troubled him. She seemed too unhappy, and he wanted to know why. While he wasn't thrilled with the prospect of their union, he had anticipated at least one of them would look forward to it. Did their ten-year age gap matter? Or was it because she'd led such a cloistered life that she found it all overwhelming? He covered her gloved hand with his own. "After the wedding, life will become more to your taste. Married ladies lead interesting, busy social lives." *While men, discontented with their marriages, seek love elsewhere*, he thought. Something he'd been determined never to do.

She nodded, her smile small.

"You do want to be married, don't you, Miss Ashton?" he inquired gently.

Her hand flew to her chest. "Oh, yes. Of course I do."

Panic was neither the emotion he expected to find in her eyes, nor what he wished for. Hugh decided not to pursue it further and turned his attention back to his horses, but he would escort her to the Kemps' garden party, which was sure to be acceptable to her mother. The Kemp's always put on a good show. Perhaps that might brighten Miss Ashton's outlook on London.

That evening, he joined Ross for dinner at their club.

Ross studied him across the table as he cut into his beef. "You seem a little subdued tonight, Hugh."

"Am I dull company? Forgive me."

"Might it have something to do with Miss Kershaw?"

Hugh stared at him. "Miss Kershaw? Lord, no. Why would you think that?"

"Her presence in London seemed to affect you."

"We met in Bath. I needed to ask her something about what happened there."

"Oh? Are you going to tell me what it was?"

"No. I can't. Sorry. Shall we call for another bottle? Have dessert? Or go to the card room?"

"Or," Ross said with a grin, "I have two ladies in mind. Sisters, and very obliging."

Hugh shook his head. "Not for me."

"No, perhaps not," Ross said with regret. "Have you heard that William Darby has set up a mistress on Jermyn Street?"

Hugh answered vaguely, disliking where this conversation was leading, and called for another bottle of claret. He had parted ways with his last mistress some months ago, wishing to be unencumbered when his wedding approached. He and the lovely widow Roslyn Enfield had enjoyed each other's company while it had lasted, but he'd hardly given her a thought since. And he suspected it was the same for Roslyn, now enjoying the company of Lord Wallace. Hugh wondered why, when he'd barely met Miss Kershaw, she still entered his mind at unexpected moments. Unaccountably annoying, when she appeared to be making the most of her situation, riding out with young Nash. But as Nash was an inveterate gambler, Hugh prayed it would go no further.

Chapter Four

AFTER MR. NASH had left her at her and the trembling maid at her aunt's door, Lucy watched him ride away before going inside. He had been quite warm toward her and made another arrangement for next week. She didn't want to see him again. Not after catching sight of a gossip sheet some lady held at a ball with the heading screaming: *Who is the mystery heiress?* It must have referred to her. And it was indisputable that a solid wall, caused by her foolish lie, stood between her and any prospective husband. Was there a way to convince them she really wasn't an heiress? But how to manage it without reflecting poorly on her family and angering her aunt? She thought of Lord Dorchester's warning. Would her family be shunned? What else could she do? She could only continue to deny it, should the matter be mentioned.

On the following Tuesday at a rout, she searched the crush of guests for the earl, but he did not attend. He was the only person with whom she could discuss her problem. But he wouldn't want anything more to do with her. And after all, what could he do to assist her?

Gentlemen wishing an introduction always sought her for dances. Many called at the house for morning tea. Lucy searched their faces but found few looked at her with any interest in her as a person, and the one who blatantly ogled her made her neck prickle. Some gentlemen were nervous and fiddled with their cravats, and one looked down his nose as if she were too far beneath him to be bothered with. Then why was he here? Another, she thought, was too brash when he spoke at length of his prowess with the reins and how he'd won a carriage race to Brighton. While her aunt presided over the tea tray and engaged the men in conversation, Lucy counted the minutes until they took their leave.

"Mr. Holcombe is an amiable gentleman," Aunt Mary said, packing away her embroidery after the last of them had departed. Her gaze settled on Lucy's face. "Didn't you find him so?"

"Mr. Holcombe?" Lucy searched through the men who had called that afternoon to recall a face. "Wasn't he the one who has a sister called Florence?"

Aunt Mary frowned. "No. That was Mr. Greenvale." With a sigh, she left her chair. "Do try to pay attention, Lucy." She shook her head. "You might make an effort to talk to them. It appears you don't *want* to be married. If that is true, why come to London?"

Lucy bit her lip as they left the drawing room. "I want to marry and have children, Aunt. It is my most fervent wish. But a relationship must begin on solid ground. And how can it when…"

"Not that business again. You made an error in judgement when faced with gossip about your father. Please put it behind you. The rumors will die down soon." She turned on the stairs with a frown. "I blame your father."

"No, Aunt, it is entirely my…" Lucy firmed her lips and followed her up the stairs.

"All is not lost, my dear." Aunt Mary's voice grew more enthused as they reached the landing. "Mr. Nash has not lost interest, and Mr. Douglas Rattray—you must remember the red-haired gentleman who danced with you at the Forster's ball—is a very engaging fellow, and much liked by the *ton*."

"Oh, yes. I remember him." The Scottish gentleman of some thirty-five years had sat talking to her aunt after he and Lucy had danced a Scotch reel, and he'd remained when she'd danced again with Mr. Greenvale. Mr. Rattray was unfailingly polite, but Lucy could not warm to him. It wasn't his appearance, exactly, although she thought him rather old, but something in his gray eyes. "He sat with you a long time, Aunt. What did you talk about?"

"I told him how difficult you have found it to fit in to London life since you came from Bath. He was most sympathetic." She slipped her arm through Lucy's as they walked to Lucy's bedchamber to change her gown. "You must admit, he is an attractive man. I was quite impressed with his interest in your welfare. I do miss your Uncle Peter's wise counsel."

Lucy regretted troubling her aunt. A prickle of unease passed down her spine. "But we don't know Mr. Rattray well. Perhaps it's best not to confide in him."

"Well, why ever not? What harm can it do, foolish girl?" She patted Lucy on the back and walked ahead of her into the bedchamber. "For a debutante from the country to have a man with such exemplary family connections interested in you is a tour de force. He tells me his brother is Baron Maitland, of Scotland."

Lucy decided she was probably being unduly cautious. And as Aunt Mary seemed confident with her judgement, she let the subject go and listened politely as her aunt spoke about their next engagement at a garden party.

"How lovely. I enjoy wandering around gardens. I used to visit the park in Bath quite often," Lucy said, trying to show some enthusiasm.

"Yes, Lord and Lady Kemp have a magnificent estate at Hampton. Wear your muslin with the lavender-blue butterflies and the bonnet with the matching ribbons. The color suits your fair complexion. Put on a spencer too if it's cool."

After luncheon two days hence, they set out in the coach for Hampton, which, with the roads so busy, proved over an hour's drive from London.

Upon arrival on the perfect spring day, they found the grounds filled with guests wandering about, enjoying the sunshine. Footmen roamed among them with trays of champagne and lemonade, and a maid followed them with platters of hors d'oeuvres.

Lucy followed Aunt Mary as she introduced her around. The reception wasn't as warm as she would have wished. She noticed the murmuring from onlookers and prayed it wasn't about her. What was it they said? That she was a fake heiress, or an heiress of some note? Worry dried her throat, so she took a good sip of the lemonade a footman had offered her.

Lucy's gaze roamed over the guests while her aunt talked to a woman in purple lace. She drew a deep breath. Lord Dorchester strolled through the gardens with an older lady on one arm, and a tall, brown-haired young woman in white muslin with a flower-decked straw bonnet on the other. It was the same young woman Lucy had seen with him in the landau at Hyde Park. She spoke to him in a familiar manner and bent to smell a red rose on a bush laden with blooms. He leaned over and plucked it, holding it out to her. She giggled and her presumed mother reprimanded him, but with a smile on her face.

Lucy told herself it didn't matter. That she had always known he wasn't free, but the thought seemed hollow and gave her no relief.

"There's Lord Dorchester," Aunt Mary said. "That must be the lady it's said he is to marry."

As usual, he was elegantly dressed. Lucy wanted to turn away before he caught her watching, but the sight of him held her captive. In that moment, he looked up and saw her. He bowed his head, his eyes meeting hers.

Her heart squeezed. Castigating herself, Lucy bobbed, then turned back to her aunt.

"And here is Mr. Rattray, who promised to join us," Aunt Mary said merrily as the smiling, red-haired gentleman strode across the lawn to them.

Lucy swallowed a groan.

He smiled at Lucy. "My, Miss Kershaw, your aunt said you were out of sorts, and you still look a little pale. I wonder what I can do to cheer you."

"It's entirely unnecessary, thank you, sir," Lucy said.

Undaunted, Mr. Rattray addressed her aunt. "Shall we view the rose arbor and then have a cup of tea?"

"Oh, yes," said Aunt Mary, "a splendid idea."

As Lucy trailed behind them, she allowed herself one more glimpse of the earl, who appeared to watch her while the two women talked together. When the young woman put a hand on his arm to gain his attention, he bent his head to listen, and he glanced back at Mr. Rattray. Might he have knowledge of Mr. Rattray her aunt should know about? Lucy wished she could ask him.

"Lucy, do keep up," Aunt Mary said. "I am growing parched in this hot sun."

⇒⟫⟨⇐

"YOU SEEM DISTRACTED," Lord Dorchester," Lady Ashton observed. "Perhaps you are not a devotee of gardens."

"Oh, Mama. Few men are I imagine," Miss Ashton said crossly. "Shall we go in?"

"I confess to a scarce knowledge of flowers," he said with a warm smile of apology for his disinterest. "Ask me about breeding sheep or horses, or cultivating land, and I'll keep you engaged for hours."

"I doubt that very much," Lady Ashton said with a wry smile.

As he escorted them into the house for afternoon tea, Hugh tried to ignore his eager response to seeing Miss Kershaw. It was downright foolish, especially with Miss Ashton standing beside him, but something he seemed to have little control over. And there was something about Rattray that gave him cause for concern, but that was none of his business. Hugh sighed inwardly as he settled the ladies at a table. He should not have been thinking of Miss Kershaw when his betrothed required his attention.

The next morning, Miss Ashton and her mother set out for home, and Hugh, with a promise to call in to see them at their neighboring property, left London the following day. His gelding, Chance, needed exercise, and he had some overdue estate matters awaiting him. Hugh also wanted to reassure himself that his mother had recovered well after her jaunt to Bath. Would he find Sarah in good spirits? Or was it too much to hope that Lord Cardew, her inexcusably casual beau, had come up to scratch?

He wanted to persuade Sarah to come and stay with him in Mayfair for a few weeks. Perhaps when facing some stiff competition, which he was sure would result when his comely sister appeared in London, Cardew might decide he wanted her for his wife, or better still, he might lose his hold over her. Although he was not Hugh's favorite choice for her, he would welcome their marriage if the man made her happy. He didn't want Sarah to be hurt, and he would be more than willing to teach him a lesson should he misbehave.

Driving his team along the tree-lined avenue toward Wood-croft, his gray stone manor house, he went over the previous day in his mind. Miss Ashton had seemed more light-hearted, but neither she nor her mother had given any indication of when, or if, they would return to London to see out the rest of the Season. Despite coming to London, he and Miss Ashton still hadn't formally announced their betrothal or set a wedding date. He wasn't sure how he felt about that. A little guilty, perhaps. But if he'd been a keener prospective bridegroom, would Miss Ashton have been different? He had tried, but some emotions couldn't be faked, especially when Miss Ashton's response was so lackluster.

Was Miss Lucy Kershaw beginning to enjoy London? Hard to tell from her small smile as she'd curtsied to him. He hoped the fuss arising from the mistaken belief in her father's prospects had died down. Some gossip was like the influenza and moved with speed through society, while some slowly filtered through. He hoped any such talk would have been dismissed before then without any new gossip to feed it. Although perhaps not among those angling for a wealthy bride. Hugh wished her well. In different circumstances, he would have taken great pleasure in rescuing her and improving their acquaintance. He recalled all too well how perfectly she'd fit into his arms on the dance floor. Small and slender, she gave the impression of delicacy, but she fought fiercely where she found injustice. The thought crept into his mind that she would be a passionate lover.

Enough of that! He urged the horses on after they'd passed through the gates to Woodcroft, and there on the far hill was the massive roof of his home above the towering, ancient trees of the park, chimneys sending curling, gray smoke above the treetops. It was always a welcome sight, with the sun setting in the west, painting the sky a myriad of colors, from aqua to purple and rose pink. He drove the curricle to the stables and left the groom to see to the horses.

Sarah awaited him at the front door with a welcoming smile. "I'm so glad to see you. We can play chess tonight. I have been utterly bored since we returned from Bath."

"Yes, I have had a pleasant journey, thank you." Hugh chucked her under the chin.

"Oh, I am horribly selfish," she admitted with a sad lack of remorse.

"I gather you haven't heard from Lord Cardew?"

"No." She bit her lip, pain in her blue eyes. "His mother holds him by the apron strings."

Hugh clamped down on his jaw. "Then can he be the right man for you?" He bristled at how badly Cardew had treated her. He wasn't good enough for Sarah, but to make too much of it would only send her into Cardew's arms.

"Oh..." She put the back of a hand to her forehead. "But I do care for him so very much."

"You are entirely too dramatic for your own good. Where is Mama?"

"She is resting."

Hugh handed his hat, coat, and gloves to a footman. "I'll change and go to her."

His mother looked pale but sat up eagerly in bed when he entered. "Darling! You must tell me all your news," she said, tidying the white, lace cap over her gray-brown locks with her fingers.

"I have nothing of much interest to relate." He sat on the edge of the bed and leaned over to kiss her cheek, breathing in her familiar violet scent.

"Oh." She looked crestfallen. "Then Miss Ashton…?"

"Nothing confirmed in that direction."

She gasped. "Why ever not? Don't they know you're the catch of the Season?"

"Are you biased?" Hugh asked with a laugh.

"Nonsense. Of course I'm not," she said affectionately. She eyed him carefully, reaching out to smooth the lapel of his coat. "What will you do?"

"I don't like to force matters, but I'll ride over and see her tomorrow." He stood. "Will you come down to dinner?"

"Of course. It isn't often we share a meal of late."

Candlelight flickered, casting a warm glow over the white, linen cloth and making the crystal sparkle. James served the fish from a silver platter, the delicate flavors scenting the air. It was good to see his mother at the dinner table again. While she and Sarah talked of what would happen once Hugh and Miss Ashton were married, his mind filled with dread at the thought of it. Seeing his betrothed again hadn't improved matters, and while he must take some of the blame for that, Miss Ashton did tend to keep him at a distance. It made him wonder why.

"You're quiet tonight, Hugh," Mama said.

Hugh raised his eyebrows. "You wish me to join in to your discussion of ladies' fashion?"

"Yes, do tell what you think of the latest bonnets," Sarah said with a laugh.

"What I know of such things you could write on the head of a pin."

"You would be more interested in the lady wearing the gown, I imagine," Sarah said cheekily.

"Sarah!" her mother admonished.

Hugh laughed. She had him there.

At noon the next day, Hugh rode Chance the six miles to the neighboring property. The Ashtons' major domo, who had been working for the estate for years, greeted him. Tyndale never seemed to age, his brown hair still without a thread of gray, although his middle had expanded and pushed at his waistcoat buttons.

"Miss Isabel is at the church, my lord."

"Thank you, Tyndale. I'll go and see her there."

It was four miles to the small, stone church on the edge of the village. When Hugh dismounted, he saw the family's trap waiting outside with the horse tugging at the grass.

He entered the shadowy interior and saw, before the altar, Miss Ashton and Mr. Benson bending over a vase of white roses, their heads close together.

Hugh gave a start. There was something disturbingly intimate about the scene. He couldn't recall noticing anything unusual between them, but he only saw them at church on Sunday. The youthful vicar, Benson, was a slender fellow, unmarried, with a pleasing, almost poetical face. Should he be paying such close attention to a young single lady in his parish?

Hugh made a lot of noise walking down the aisle.

They both looked up and stepped away.

"My lord?" Mr. Benson said, coming toward him, his face wreathed in smiles. "How good to see you."

Hugh nodded. "Mr. Benson."

"Lord Dorchester, Mr. Benson was admiring my roses. I picked them this morning. The dew is still on the petals." Miss

Ashton looked flustered, her cheeks pink and her eyes bright. Hugh had never seen her like this in his company. Was there something here he should know about? "Come home to tea? Mama would love to see you."

"Certainly." He held out his arm to her and escorted her back down the aisle.

"Shall we see you at church on Sunday, my lord?" Mr. Benson called.

"If I'm not called back to London." Hugh touched his hat. "Good day, Vicar."

After a quick glance at the vicar, who remained, watching them leave with a troubled frown, Miss Ashton accompanied Hugh from the church.

"What went on there, Miss Ashton?" he asked, once they were outside and out of earshot.

Her hazel eyes looked worried before she glanced away. "Nothing. Why do you ask? The vicar and I share an interest in plants."

Hugh nodded and helped her into the trap before untying the reins attached to a post. Had he imagined something between them? Instinct told him it would be unwise to pursue it. He might hurt her or force her to tell him. Whatever Miss Ashton felt for the fellow, the family would never agree to such a marriage. But the time would come, and soon, when Hugh and his prospective bride must address their feelings and settle this between them.

Chapter Five

MR. RATTRAY JOINED Aunt Mary and Lucy at every function they attended. He dined with them at a Mayfair hotel and escorted them to the Theatre Royal to see the famous actor Edmund Kean play Shylock. Lucy was enthralled by the actor's expressive eyes and convincing performance. While Mr. Rattray seldom addressed Lucy, except for polite inquiries as to her health and whether she enjoyed the play, she often sensed his gaze measuring her. Was he interested in marrying Aunt Mary and feared Lucy would cause him trouble? But why should she? She would take pleasure in seeing her aunt happy again. Aunt Mary disliked widowhood and welcomed a man's attention. Lucy wished she could approve of Mr. Rattray. Yet the more she saw of him, the less she trusted him, although she admitted to having no reason for the feeling. He had done nothing to deserve her suspicion. However, the impression grew stronger each time she was in his company. To suggest that to her aunt without proof would only upset Aunt Mary and make her rightfully angry, so Lucy kept silent.

The following week, they attended another ball. When she entered the dance floor on Mr. Nash's arm, Lord Dorchester and a pretty, young woman with light-brown ringlets joined their set. She was not the same lady Lucy had seen with him at the garden party and on the carriage ride. Lucy tried to give her attention to the steps of the quadrille, but inevitably, when the earl took his place beside Lucy and her dance partner, she forgot everything but him.

"Miss Kershaw. Mr. Nash." Lord Dorchester introduced his partner, a Miss Ely, who smiled engagingly.

"Miss Ely. My lord." When Mr. Nash rose from his bow, flustered, he stumbled over his feet as he proceeded down the line.

"Enjoying the ball, Miss Kershaw?" Lord Dorchester asked, when next they came together.

"Yes, very much, my lord."

"I was right," Mr. Nash whispered when he returned to her side. "Dorchester has taken note of me. Wouldn't you say so?"

"Of course," Lucy said promptly.

The dance ended, and she and Mr. Nash joined the orderly line to leave the dance floor. After Nash had left her, Lord Dorchester and another young lady with darker hair came over to Lucy.

"Miss Kershaw. Might I have a moment? Sarah, this is Miss Lucy Kershaw. Miss Kershaw, this is my sister, Lady Sarah Fairburn. She has expressed a desire to meet you." Lord Dorchester turned toward the young woman beside him. "As debutantes, perhaps you'll find much in common."

Lucy bobbed, very surprised that an earl's daughter, who smiled graciously, wanted to meet her.

"Would you care to sit with me until the next dance is called, Miss Kershaw?"

"I would, thank you, Lady Sarah."

Lord Dorchester bowed and left them. After telling her aunt, who looked pleased, Lucy joined Lady Sarah, and they sat together watching the noisy, chatting crowd traversing the rim of the ballroom floor.

"Mama is talking to friends." Lady Sarah raised her voice above the din and gestured with her fan toward the far row of seats where several ladies sat chatting together. The dowager countess was recognizable by her blue eyes and dark-brown hair the same color as her son's and daughter's. She was deathly pale. Had she suffered from an illness? "She rarely comes to London and is catching up on news."

Lady Sarah's natural manner soon put Lucy at ease. She was slender to the point of thinness, her sharp collarbones revealed by the neckline of her gown with a thin, rather delicate face. Her best features were her abundant dark-brown hair and stunning light-blue eyes, much like her brother's. "Tell me about yourself, Miss Kershaw. Where do you hail from?"

"Bath, my lady."

"Ah, yes, Bath. My mother and I have just returned from there. We enjoyed the entertainments in the town. How blessed you are to have grown up in such a vibrant city."

"It is a busy, interesting place," Lucy agreed, although she hadn't been able to enjoy many of the functions. But she and her good friend, Alice Graham, rode together and shopped on the Pulteney Bridge. They enjoyed tea and buns at Sally Lunn's shop, but not since Alice had married and given birth to a daughter.

"The Kentish countryside where I grew up is pretty, but a trifle dull. Apart from the dances at the assembly hall and dining with the neighbors, there's little to do. But I love to ride." Lady Sarah laughed. "Mama had a terrible time making me abandon my horse, Beauty, to attend my lessons."

"I love horses." Lucy had ridden in Bath but had never owned a horse, although she'd often yearned for one.

"We might ride together in Rotten Row. My brother doesn't keep a suitable horse in London, so I shall hire one."

"I must do the same." Lucy wondered what Aunt Mary would think of that.

"Then let's meet at the Hyde Park stables. Is Sunday morning, after church, suitable?"

"I must ask my aunt. But if she gives her permission, it would be most agreeable."

As they talked, the gulf between their rank in life seemed to matter a little less. Lucy relaxed until Lady Sarah mentioned her brother. "Did you meet in Bath?" Curiosity widened her lovely, light-blue eyes.

"Merely a few words in passing," Lucy said carefully. "And we danced once at a ball here in London."

"You danced with Hugh?" Lady Sarah's gaze became speculative. "Fancy. My brother said he wasn't fond of dancing, but he seems to have changed his mind. But this is my first time here, so I daresay I shall discover more about him." She sighed. "Brothers seem to keep their thoughts and feelings close to their chest. I've always wanted a sister to talk to. Do you have a brother or sister?"

"No."

"How sad for you."

Lucy nodded, not sure how to reply. Perhaps if she had a brother, or sister, she might not have worried so much about Papa.

Their partners made their way through the crowded ballroom to them when the last dance was announced.

Lucy stood, disappointed that their conversation had been cut short.

"I shall look for you at Hyde Park on Sunday," Lady Sarah said. "Shall we say, eleven o'clock, before the rush?"

"Yes. I hope to be there."

"You must come to tea afterward. I'm sure Mama would like to meet you."

They parted company as Lucy puzzled over her invitation. Surely, the dowager countess wouldn't have been interested in meeting her? Probably Lady Sarah was merely being polite. But Lucy liked her natural, friendly manner, which was a contrast to that of many of the standoffish debutantes. She hoped Aunt Mary would approve of her riding without an escort. She didn't want to take her aunt's grumpy groom with her. Surely, Lady Sarah's groom would suffice for both of them. Fortunately, the seamstress had altered her cousin Anabel's discarded blue riding habit, which included a smart, military-styled jacket piped with gold braid. It was flattering, and this was Lucy's chance to wear it.

She hoped to hear more about Lord Dorchester, whose Christian name was Hugh, she'd learned, from Lady Sarah. What had he been like as a boy? Had he gotten into scrapes? Had he always been so even-tempered? He exuded confidence and would probably act quickly and forcefully if someone dared slight him. She thirsted for all those details about him. Anyone would be curious about such a man, she reasoned, as she and Mr. Greenvale joined the dancers on the floor. She gazed over the crowded ballroom for a sign of him.

"You are contemplative tonight, Miss Kershaw," Mr. Greenvale said, his smile wooden.

Lucy gathered her wits. She was being rude, so she smiled broadly, causing him to stroke a hand over his hair. "A little weary, sir, but never too tired to dance."

As the dance came to a close, Lucy couldn't resist one last lingering look at the earl. When she spied him laughing at something some gentleman had said, her heart beat faster, but she wasn't sure if it was from the energetic dance, or the earl.

ON SUNDAY, AFTER they'd returned from church, Aunt Mary ferreted out a dashing black riding hat with a feather for Lucy to wear. "Do you know how to choose a suitable hack?" she asked, suddenly concerned. "I shall have my groom advise you."

"I'm sure Lady Sarah's groom will accompany her," Lucy said. "He can help me."

"Mm. I suppose that is in order. Spencer will drive you to the park and make sure her ladyship's groom is there before he leaves you. My, that hat does suit you." She gave the brim a tug. "Come to the mirror and look for yourself."

After looking at the mirror, Lucy agreed. The graceful hat

was very stylish. Excitement tightened her chest. Would this be the first occasion where she could enjoy herself and not have to worry about the possible consequences of her lie?

⟫⟫⟫⟪⟪⟪

SARAH PAUSED IN buttering her toast to level a glance at Hugh seated across the breakfast table from her. "I heard you danced with Miss Kershaw a week or two ago."

"It's my duty to dance with a debutante. I believe you asked me to invite your friend Miss Ely to dance the quadrille."

"But I didn't ask you to dance with Miss Kershaw, did I?"

He raised his eyebrows. "Who is also a debutante. So?"

"So..." She grinned. "You selected the prettiest one at the ball."

"Was she? I recognized her from Bath. That's why I chose her."

"Ha!"

He rubbed his neck. "Tell me, did you enjoy your first ball?"

"It was as I expected," Sarah said. "Noisy, smoky, and everyone watching everyone else and talking behind their backs."

"That's a cynical view to have. What is the reason?"

She shrugged her thin shoulders.

He glanced at her breakfast, which consisted of one slice of toast. Sarah had lost weight. Dash it all, he'd swear Lord Cardew was the reason. "Did you have a partner for every dance?"

"I am an earl's daughter. Of course men pursue me."

"You aren't fair to yourself. You're a pretty girl."

"Oh, Hugh. I am not."

"You are too thin. You eat little more than a bird," he said, giving in to the desire to advise her, although he feared it would not be welcome.

She nodded, studied her toast, and said nothing.

"Will you try to improve your diet while here in London?"

She shrugged. "If you wish."

"Good. No time like the present." He turned to the footman standing beside the sideboard laden with hot food in chaffing dishes. "Benjamin, serve Lady Sarah with some eggs and bacon. Kedgeree too. And more toast."

Her eyes widened. "I can't eat all that, Hugh."

"Do your best. My chef will make anything you fancy." He smiled, pleased to have at least her vague promise.

Sarah stared at the loaded plate Benjamin put before her. At Hugh's urging to eat before it grew cold, she forked up some egg. "Miss Kershaw is nice. I like her. We are to ride together on Sunday in Hyde Park if her aunt agrees."

"You'll require an escort. I'll join you."

She grinned. "I thought you would."

He laughed. "Minx. Are you trying to interfere in my affairs?"

"I wouldn't dare."

She was the picture of innocence. Tit for tat. Time to take a more active part in Sarah's affairs. He would invite Luke Beaufort to join them on Sunday. An earl's second son, he was a good-looking fellow, here in London to find a wife. And more importantly, Hugh liked him a great deal. Luke could more than hold a candle to Sarah's beau, Lord Cardew. He'd eclipse him.

Hugh pushed a dish of jam toward Sarah, who had put down her knife and fork. "More tea for Lady Sarah and coffee for me, Benjamin."

During the week, he was pleased to observe Sarah eating more at meals, although he was careful not to mention it. She still appeared too nervous for his liking. Was it Cardew, or their mother's health, or both?

On Sunday, Hugh and Sarah traveled to the stables in Hyde Park to choose mounts. In the curricle, he paved the way, stirring her gentle heart by relating Luke's tragic story: the fire which had destroyed his house and claimed his pregnant wife. "Luke has restored the building. He has plans to marry," he said.

Sarah sighed. "That is so sad."

"It is. But he hasn't let it sink him into the depths, and he has hopes for the future." Hugh eyed her and continued, thinking Sarah had taken the lure like the salmon in the river at home.

"I know what you're about, Hugh." Sarah briskly smoothed her doeskin gloves. "But I doubt I could consider anyone else in my life. It's always been Robert."

"Keep an open mind, Sarah. I think you'll like him," Hugh said, refusing to be discouraged as the coach pulled up at the stables and the groom put down the steps.

Miss Kershaw soon joined them, looking wonderful in dark blue and a dashing riding hat.

"Lord Dorchester, I didn't expect you to accompany us."

"I hope it pleases you to have my company, Miss Kershaw."

She blushed. "But of course. I must tell the driver that all is well." She turned and hurried back to the waiting carriage.

As the ladies chatted, Hugh roamed the stables, smelling of saddle oil, hay, and manure. He disliked hiring horses, which were often a disappointing ride, and some were bad-tempered, but he hadn't brought Chance to the city this Season. He chose two mares, a roan and a gray for the ladies, and was inspecting the fetlock of a chestnut gelding for himself when Luke arrived. Tall and broad across the shoulders, he looked well in riding garb.

Hugh went to introduce Luke to the ladies. "I don't believe you've met my sister, Lady Sarah," he said. He was gratified to note Sarah's slight flush as she greeted the handsome fellow.

Encouraged that his idea might bear fruit, Hugh decided to let nature take its course. He turned his attention to Miss Kershaw.

Hugh approached the young lady, who stood beside the gray horse. "May I help you mount, Miss Kershaw?" Breathing in her fragrance, redolent of lilies, his hands at her waist sent a shock of awareness through him. It felt amazing just to touch her through her habit, and the sensation brought all sorts of ribald thoughts to his mind.

"Thank you, Lord Dorchester."

He thought she looked a little flustered as he turned to mount his horse. Did she sense the strong attraction between them? He had never felt this way with a lady fully-clothed. Had never felt this way at all, he realized.

Luke cupped his hands to boost Sarah into the saddle, then he mounted his own horse. Hugh noticed how Sarah watched Luke approvingly. Now, if only Luke might show some interest in Sarah, but there was no sign of that beyond a friendly politeness.

Early days, Hugh told himself. Astride a horse, Luke was an impressive figure. The perfect man to banish Cardew from her mind.

They left the stables and their horses trotted across the grass.

At this time of day, Rotten Row was quiet, as most riders either came earlier, or later in the early evening. Few carriages drove along the South Carriage Drive, except for a high-perched phaeton driven by a dashing young blade. Hugh recognized him. Nash. He raised his crop to salute him, but the young man's eyes were on Miss Kershaw, deep in conversation as she rode beside Sarah.

Hugh tightened his jaw. Surely it was concern, not jealousy he felt. Although her response to Nash was not his affair, the man was not the right sort for Miss Kershaw. But that was not something he was able to tell her.

Riding beside Luke, Hugh glanced behind him. Miss Kershaw responded to Nash's greeting with a casual wave, before turning back to Sarah again. At any rate, she didn't appear to be in love with the fellow. His deep sense of relief and the extraordinary feeling she caused in him left him baffled. The only answer was that he felt protective of her. It was not only remarkable, but uncharacteristic of him. And he was pretty sure he was fooling himself. *Let it alone*, he thought. He wasn't free.

But he couldn't help riding over to join her, which served the dual purpose to having Luke join Sarah.

When Miss Kershaw turned to him, he was surprised to see worry darken her eyes.

"I hope you approve of me befriending Lady Sarah, Lord Dorchester."

"Why would I not?" he asked, startled.

She shrugged and tightened her hands on the reins, causing the horse to sidle. "Because of the gossip about me."

"Is there gossip about you?"

She frowned at him. "You must know I refer to my lie about my father."

"I had forgotten it," he said. "I can see it is not your habit to tell lies."

She gazed at him for a moment, her big, brown eyes regarding him. "You are too good." Then she urged her horse into a canter to catch up with Luke and Sarah.

Too good? It was not how he thought of himself when his hands clasped her slim waist, and a rush of very different thoughts filled his mind and stirred his blood.

Chapter Six

STONE WALLS ENCLOSED Lord Dorchester's magnificent Mayfair mansion, which nestled in a lush garden filled with bright spring flowers. In the drawing room, Lucy sipped tea from a delicate floral cup while seated on a cream satin armchair opposite Lady Sarah and her mother, the Dowager Countess of Dorchester. Somewhere Lucy had never expected to find herself, even in her wildest dreams. She should have felt like a fraud. But Lord Dorchester knew the truth about her and could have refused to allow his sister to befriend her if he wished, and despite that, she was enjoying herself too much to care.

Lord Dorchester's footman had taken a note to Aunt Mary and Mr. Beaufort had driven Lucy and Lady Sarah in his carriage to his lordship's home. After which, disappointingly, Lord Dorchester and Mr. Beaufort had disappeared into the library.

Lucy felt the dowager countess's gaze upon her and straightened her back. Was the elegant lady aware of the lie? Lucy must not think of it, or her hand would tremble. She carefully replaced her cup on its saucer. She was acutely conscious that she did not belong among these people. But Lady Sarah was so warm and reassuring, drawing Lucy into the conversation by recalling the sight of a very fat man on a small horse riding down the Row.

"*Sarah!*" Lady Dorchester frowned. "You should not make fun of people."

"But, Mama, he was whipping the poor horse." She grinned at Lucy. "Miss Kershaw rode up to him and chastised him."

The dowager countess turned to Lucy, eyebrows raised, no doubt thinking she lacked manners. "Sarah tells me you grew up in Bath, Miss Kershaw."

"Yes, my lady."

"Do you still have family there?"

"Only my father."

"I seem to remember meeting the Marquess of Berwick some years ago. The Kershaws hail from the far north. Might they be relatives of yours?"

Lucy tensed, fearing exposure. "Yes, they are distant relatives."

The dowager countess nodded, then rose from her chair. "I'll rest, Sarah, and take luncheon in my room. I'll leave you to entertain your guest. Good bye, Miss Kershaw." She nodded to Lucy and, looking thin and rather fragile, drifted from the room, her shawl trailing from her shoulders.

Lady Sarah watched her mother with concern darkening her eyes. "Mama has been unwell," she said in a low voice. "She keeps better health in the country. Hugh wished for her to remain there and allow him to chaperone me. She should rest after our sojourn to Bath. But she does enjoy a little social life." She stood. "Will you stay for luncheon?"

"My aunt will expect me at home," Lucy said.

"No matter. We'll send a message advising her of it."

Why was Lady Sarah so intent on having her here? Perhaps it was because, as a new debutante, she lacked friends in London? It seemed difficult to believe. "Then I should like to have luncheon with you. Thank you, my lady."

Lady Sarah pulled the bell rope.

Lord Dorchester and Mr. Beaufort joined them at a long table in the formal dining room. The walls in the room featured Delft blue floral wallpaper and swags of gold damask at the windows. Gilt-framed mirrors and paintings hung on the walls, and an impressive crystal chandelier hovered overhead.

Lucy enjoyed their company. Lady Sarah and her brother traded quips, talking about growing up in Kent, fascinating Lucy, and making Mr. Beaufort laugh.

"Bragging about your prowess as a mountaineer, you climbed the apple tree to fetch me the best apple, then fell and broke your arm." Lady Sarah's eyes filled with mirth.

"The branch broke." His lordship cocked an eyebrow. "Such gratitude," he remarked, but a smile tugged at his lips.

The brother and sister were obviously on very good terms. It made Lucy wish she'd had a sibling, but her mother had died before the family had grown any larger, and her father had never remarried. He had loved Mama dearly and put flowers on her grave every Sunday after church. How she missed him. Was he well? If he had lost money at card play, his spirits would plummet.

The spread surpassed the usual offerings at her aunt's table. A platter of salad, cold meats, and chicken plus a selection of breads, cheeses, and exotic fruits. At the conclusion of the meal, footmen served aromatic coffee in the drawing room.

Lady Sarah put down her coffee cup. "Shall we play a game of shuttlecock?"

"On a full stomach?" Lord Dorchester leaned back in his chair, a hand on his flat stomach.

She grinned. "Sorry. I forgot you were almost in your dotage."

"Right. I'll partner you, Miss Kershaw," her brother said promptly, nodding at Lucy. "I require your help to teach my impertinent sister a lesson."

Lucy tried not to be nervous as they filed out into the spring sunshine. Servants set up the net on the small lawn. She had never played the game, but she'd certainly give it her best and hope not to disgrace herself.

Lucy quickly picked up the rules and discovered she had an aptitude for the game. After Lady Sarah had missed a shot, Lord

Dorchester and Lucy were winning. Keen not to let her partner down, she lunged for the shuttlecock when it sailed over the net. She stumbled on the uneven grass and thudded down onto her bottom.

Lord Dorchester was at her side in an instant, concern in his eyes. "Are you all right, Miss Kershaw? You haven't turned an ankle?"

"No, my lord," she said, silently rebuking herself for her clumsiness.

His arm around her, he helped her to stand. His warm, clean male sweat and musky cologne lingered before he moved away. She was certain her face glowed like an oil lamp, and she took several quick breaths.

Lord Dorchester turned to the footman standing nearby. "Bring a glass of lemonade for Miss Kershaw."

Lucy shook her head. "Really, I'm perfectly all right."

"You look a little flushed," Lady Sarah said. "A cool drink will help. Please bring lemonade for all of us, James."

As Lucy apologized to Lady Sarah for spoiling their game, she caught the lady's expression when she glanced at her brother. Shocked, Lucy recognized the gleam in her eyes as satisfaction. Was Lady Sarah attempting to bring her brother and Lucy together? But why? Did she not approve of his betrothed? Might she have heard the gossip about the inheritance and considered the supposed heiress a suitable bride for her brother? Lucy's stomach twisted at the thought. But she could have been wrong. There was really no way of knowing why she'd been welcomed as if she were one of them.

The footman returned with a tray of lemonade and offered it around. Lucy sipped hers, glad of the cool drink. She wanted to hold the glass against her hot cheeks. It was a sunny day, but a fresh spring breeze stirred the leaves of the trees in the garden. "I must return home before Aunt Mary sends someone to find me." She smiled shakily and returned the empty glass to the footman's tray.

"I'll take you," Lord Dorchester said promptly.

"Yes, take good care of Miss Kershaw, Hugh," Lady Sarah said. "A maid will accompany you. Shall we go in, Mr. Beaufort?"

"I'd best be getting along too," he replied.

"Yes, of course." Lady Sarah's smile looked forced. "A footman will bring your carriage around." It made Lucy regret having spoiled their game.

"I've enjoyed the day, and the company." With a smile that rested for a moment on Lady Sarah, and a small bow, Mr. Beaufort left them.

Lucy considered him attractive, although somewhat restrained, and it was obvious Lady Sarah thought so too, for she was clearly disappointed that he hadn't joined her, as she watched him climb into his carriage.

"Shall we see you at the Williams' card party on Thursday?" Lady Sarah asked.

"I'm not sure of my aunt's plans," Lucy admitted. "But I hope to."

"Do try to come," Lady Sarah said as the carriage appeared. Lord Dorchester settled Lucy and the maid, whose name was Annie, into it, leaped aboard and took up the reins.

The matched pair of grays moved in unison over the cobbles as they continued down to Hyde Park Corner through the leafy Mayfair streets, past carriages and pedestrians in fashionable attire.

The traffic grew heavier, and they came to a stop as carriages, coaches and wagons tried to make their way through the narrow streets, the pavements crowded with pedestrians some of whom bravely attempted to cross the road.

As the carriage inched forward, they were held up again by a crossing sweeper.

Lord Dorchester turned to her, his blue gaze sweeping over her, the reins held lightly in his large, capable hands. "No discernable effects from your fall?"

She brushed her habit skirts. "Only a small grass stain and

wounded pride."

He laughed, then met another snarl in the traffic ahead as they entered St. James's Park caught his attention. "Nonsense. You played very well," he said when he turned back to her.

The difference between Aunt Mary's townhouse and the earl's mansion was considerable. Lucy must not forget that he came from a different world. Lucy glanced at his noble profile as he guided the horses around a sedan chair. She still couldn't fathom why they had included her in their circle of friends, but she feared both Lady Sarah and her mother believed she was an heiress. There seemed no other reason. The truth of her simple upbringing in a small house with only two servants would surely shock them.

"Do you know of a Mr. Rattray?" Lucy hoped to learn more while in his company. She might not get the chance again.

He turned to look at her, his dark eyebrows raised. "I do, but not well. Why do you ask?"

"I think he plans to marry my aunt. I must confess I don't like him, although I cannot say why."

"There's not much known about him, as he hails from Scotland," he said. "Would you like me to find out more about him?"

She smiled, feeling foolish. "No, thank you. I am probably being unfair to him. And I could not interfere. My aunt seems lonely. I want her to be happy."

He pulled up outside her aunt's townhouse, tied off the reins and sat for a moment, looking at her. "You're a sympathetic soul, Miss Kershaw."

She flushed under his scrutiny. "Actually, my father says I'm too outspoken."

The warm expression in his eyes couldn't possibly have been desire.

His gaze drifted to her mouth and for a moment, she thought he might kiss her, her pulse thudding. Surely, he wouldn't kiss her with the maid looking on. While she wanted him to with all her heart, she knew it was wrong. He was betrothed. But the impulse was so strong, she feared if he did, she would not push him away.

She held herself still as he trailed a finger along her jaw, then with an intake of breath, turned away and the moment passed.

He jumped from the phaeton and came around to her. Reaching up, he lifted her down. For a moment, she stopped breathing as her breasts brushed against the hard wall of his chest. A hot tingle shot through her nipples. He placed her on her feet and stepped away. Very much aware of him, Lucy couldn't look up, fearing what she would see in his eyes would echo her feelings. He belonged to another and there was the scandal hanging over her head. If anything happened between them, she could only hurt him as well as herself.

She sensed the strength in him, when he clasped her hand to help her negotiate the step and walked with her to the door.

He rapped the door knocker, then stood back from her and cleared his throat. "I must apologize to your aunt for keeping you so long."

"No, please don't bother," she said, her voice sounding strained. Aunt Mary would read too much into it. It would be hard enough for her to make light of her friendship with Lady Sarah, as it was. If her aunt suspected an attraction existed between Lord Dorchester and herself, the fuss it would cause! Lucy would be forced to return to Bath.

She watched the play of emotions on his face, mirroring hers, then he turned swiftly away. "Good bye, Miss Kershaw."

"Good bye. And thank you," she called after him. Her heart still beating too fast, she remained to admire his lean, athletic body as he jumped effortlessly back into the phaeton. He turned his magnificent horses in a neat half circle and continued back along the road. Lucy felt a little shaky. As if something monumental had happened. If he had kissed her, it could mean only one thing. He wanted her for his mistress. She wasn't sure how she would have responded. Being with him made her feel safe, despite her common sense telling her there was no such thing as safety and certainly not with a man about to marry someone else.

She considered being a mistress beneath her and hoped he would never ask her. It would ruin her good opinion of him.

As she entered the house, the clasp of his long-fingered hand lingered, warm and strong. Would she see him again? It had been wonderful to spend those few hours with him and Lady Sarah. But this only made it harder to forget him when faced with the harsh reality of her past, which must soon catch up with her.

In low spirits, Lucy entered the drawing room, and saw her cousin Anabel seated on the sofa with a box of chocolates in her lap. A pretty, plump young woman with a round face, light-brown hair, and blue eyes, her gaze sharp as she greeted Lucy.

Lucy sat beside her. "How nice to see you at last, Anabel. Where is Aunt Mary?"

"Mr. Rattray has driven her to the park," Anabel said, taking in Lucy's clothes. "You are wearing my old habit. The material is of excellent quality, but the military style will go out of fashion now the war had ended."

"I am grateful for it, Anabel. Thank you."

Anabel popped a chocolate between her small, rosebud lips. "That blue is better suited to someone with blue eyes," she said as she chewed. "You would look better in green."

Lucy resisted asking her if she had an old green one to offer.

"I was often told how flattering blue was for my coloring," Anabel continued. "My new habit is sky-blue and the very latest fashion. Although I rarely ride since I married."

"I am looking forward to meeting your husband."

Her cousin's mouth pulled down in a sulk. "Howe is always very busy. He's in parliament, you know."

"Yes. I did…"

"He's very much respected."

"I'm sure he is." Lucy rose, anxious to bring this uncomfortable conversation to an end. "I must go up and change."

"You missed luncheon. I came expecting to see you."

"I'm sorry." Lucy forced a smile. "I went riding with Lady Sarah Fairburn and Lord Dorchester in Rotten Row and had luncheon with them at his home."

"How fancy," Anabel said flatly. She stood, and ordering the skirts of her pink-and-white-striped morning gown, crossed to the mirror over the fireplace. She peered into it, wiping chocolate from her mouth with her handkerchief.

"We can talk more when I come down." Lucy waited for an answer at the door.

Still at the mirror, Anabel said, "I doubt I'll be here. I'm going to Bond Street to buy a new bonnet."

Lucy smiled. "Trying on hats is fun."

"What is Lord Dorchester like?" Anabel asked as Lucy opened the door.

Everything in a man a woman would wish for. "Kind, and generous."

"He must be," Anabel called after her. "To have invited you into his home."

Rolling her eyes, Lucy shut the door and climbed the stairs, thinking how much nicer Jane was than her sister. But something was amiss with Anabel. She'd looked quite miserable when her husband's name was mentioned.

Lucy put a hand on her chest to slow her breathing. Love made one so vulnerable and often seemed to cause heartache rather than happiness. She frowned and tried to tamp down her impossible attraction to Lord Dorchester.

WHEN HUGH ARRIVED home, his thoughts remained on Miss Kershaw. Her fresh, lily of the valley scent, how her curvy body had felt beneath his hands at the park when he'd assisted her onto her horse. And again while driving her home. How her eyes had gazed into his, seeking advice. That he desired her was no surprise. But the force of it was. Being close to her set his blood afire. Hugh wanted to gather her into his arms, to kiss her lush lips and chase the worry and uncertainty from her eyes. While he couldn't do that, he did intend to make inquiries about Mr. Rattray, whom he felt sure was not as he appeared.

When he walked into the house, Sarah hovered in the hall. She smiled brightly at him. "A pleasant day, was it not?"

"Indeed."

She followed him to the library. "I find Mr. Beaufort interesting. He has lovely manners."

Hugh fought not to smile as he opened the library door. "He's a genuinely decent man. Come in and have a glass of ratafia."

Once he'd poured their drinks, he sat and turned the subject to Miss Kershaw. "You seem taken with her, Sarah."

"I like her very much. She is not top-lofty at all for an heiress."

"Where did you hear that bit of gossip?"

She frowned. "A woman at the ball told me. Why?"

He groaned inwardly. It appeared the gossip had spread through London. "It's merely a rumor. I doubt it's true, as Miss Kershaw herself denies it."

"Oh." Sarah shrugged. "I still like her."

"Good."

She narrowed her eyes. "And you do too, do you not?"

"There is nothing to dislike," he said cautiously.

"You were keen to drive her home," she said with a sly smile.

He handed her the glass of ratafia and turned back to the sideboard to pour himself a glass of Madeira. "Should I have asked her to walk?"

She laughed. "You know what I mean."

"Miss Kershaw is comely, and being betrothed doesn't render a fellow blind."

As Hugh took a seat, his sister frowned. "How are things between you and Miss Ashton?"

"Not as good as I would like. I have a problem I'm not sure how to deal with."

"What is it?"

Hugh contemplated whether it was a good idea to disclose what he had witnessed. It was not something he would have done previously. He had never expressed his feelings openly. He thought that his emotions were less intense than most people's because of his upbringing. Gentlemen were taught from an early age to appear aloof from unruly emotions. And while he had sought out women he'd found attractive, he'd never developed deep feelings for any of them.

He and Miss Ashton had been neighbors since childhood. Could he have let her down by failing to pursue her passionately? Had a vicar answered her need for more than Hugh had been prepared to give?

It was surprising, but since meeting Miss Kershaw, his views on life seemed to have changed. She'd given him a glimpse of what might be. And he would very much like to have it for himself.

Hugh pushed those unsettling thoughts away. It didn't matter what he might come to feel for Miss Kershaw with her passionate soul. He had to at least attempt to win Miss Ashton's affections and accept their marriage as his future.

As he considered telling Sarah, he finished his wine. She could exhibit sound good sense. And she was the only one he could discuss this with. They needed airing, for doubts had crept in. Was he wrong about the scene in the church? Had he understood Miss Ashton and the vicar to be closer than they actually were?

"The vicar?" Sarah looked astonished after he'd described what he'd seen. "It sounds odd to me that she would undertake such a task. It's my understanding that older or married ladies arrange the flowers for the church."

"Miss Ashton denied anything occurred. But if she cares for the vicar, it explains her reluctance to come to London for the Season."

"What about her parents? Wouldn't they urge her to make her debut?"

"She is to attend the queen's drawing room in July. But I suspect Sir Phillip and Lady Ashton prefer her to remain in the country until then. Her mother is keen for her to live close by. And if Miss Ashton comes to London, who knows what might happen?"

"What a mess." Sarah raised her glass to her lips. "You should extricate yourself from the betrothal. Since you were never involved in the decision, it wouldn't be seen as unethical. Besides, few people in London are aware of it. There may be vague rumors, but you've made no official announcement. And Miss Ashton has yet to come out."

"But what would happen to Miss Ashton should I renege on the promise made between her father and mine? Her parents will be furious, not only with me, but also with her." He shook his head. "It would not be honorable."

Sarah shrugged. "She can marry her vicar. Not everyone is well suited to handle a countesses's responsibilities."

"If only it were that simple." Hugh finished his wine and put down the glass. He must talk to Miss Ashton. Convince her they would be happy together, although he had yet to convince himself of it. "If Mama is well enough to remain in London as your chaperone, I'll drive down to Kent." He raked his fingers through his hair. "This conversation with Miss Ashton is long overdue."

"I'm sure Mama will be pleased, should you tell her. It will relieve her, in fact. Don't worry. I'll make sure she gets plenty of rest."

Hugh nodded. "I'll leave the day after the Williams' card party. You can attend that party with me."

Sarah's eyes brightened. "I may play cards?"

"Yes, but don't lose all my money."

She glared at him. "I intend to win."

"Not so easy among those seasoned players."

"Ye of little faith," she scoffed.

He wondered what Miss Ashton would have to say. She had

denied anything was wrong. But it hadn't been a forceful denial. Would she wish to continue as before? Or was she prepared to be honest and work with him to end it? Her parents must take into consideration her chance for a happy future, as well as his.

Hugh gritted his teeth. It had never been his wish to enter into an arranged marriage. While he must produce an heir at some point, love was the only reason to tie oneself down for life to one woman. And he'd prefer the freedom to choose her himself.

Chapter Seven

"WE SHALL ATTEND the Williams' card party," Aunt Mary declared after Lucy had mentioned Lady Sarah would be there. "I'll send our acceptance." She rose from the morning room sofa and, ordering her skirts, strode toward the door.

Lucy doubted it was her aunt's first choice for tomorrow evening's entertainment.

"You must encourage your friendship with Lady Sarah," her aunt said. "Jane and Anabel will accompany us. It is advantageous for your cousins to have such important connections."

Her association with Lady Sarah had certainly raised Lucy from a disappointing niece to one with good prospects. She hoped her aunt wouldn't be too disappointed when their friendship waned, because once Sarah became betrothed to a titled gentleman, their lives would go in different directions, although it made Lucy sad to think it. She liked Lady Sarah a good deal.

"Mr. Rattray might accompany us. I'm sure he has received an invitation. No one shuts the door on that gentleman," her aunt cooed. "I shall write to him."

Aunt Mary left Lucy alone with her thoughts. When she'd failed to supply any answers to her problem that satisfied her, Lucy picked up the book she was currently reading, and taking up her shawl, opened the glass-paned doors to the garden. A cherry tree laden with pink blossoms grew in the center of the small lawn.

Breathing in the bloom's delicate scent, Lucy sat on the near-by garden seat. She delighted in the few occasions she could sit in the sun and read, and that was precisely what she intended to do. She opened her library book and was soon absorbed in the story. Lucy heard the door behind her open but didn't turn to see who it was. She was enthralled when Marianne fell down and sprained her ankle and the dashing Willoughby carried her home on his horse.

"Well, what a picture you make beneath the flowering tree," came a jocular voice. "May I join you?"

She reluctantly closed her book and gazed up at Mr. Rattray. "My aunt is upstairs writing a letter to you," she said. "Has the maid informed her you are here, sir?"

"No. A footman let me in. When I saw you through the glass doors, I thought to myself, *How lonely and troubled she looks.* So I've come to cheer you."

Lucy squirmed. "I am neither of those things, sir. I enjoy reading."

He smiled, undaunted by the snub, and held out his hand. "May I see?"

She could do nothing other than hand the book to him.

"Ah. *Sense and Sensibility.* 'By a lady,' it says here." He looked up. "A romantic tale? Young women are invariably romantic."

"I am told I am quite practical." Lucy held out her hand. He closed the book and handed it to her.

He moistened his lips with his tongue. "My, not only lovely, but also intelligent."

Lucy stood abruptly and gathered up her shawl and book. "I'll go in. My aunt must be wondering where I am."

His hand on her arm made her skin crawl. "You don't like me, Miss Kershaw. Have I done something to deserve this coldness?"

Lucy's conscience pricked. She had no reason to be so abrupt except for her instincts. She forced a smile. "Of course not. I do beg your pardon if that is how it appeared." She turned toward the house, forcing him to drop his hand. "We must go in search of my aunt. I know she will want to see you."

"Of course," he said flatly.

Aunt Mary must have spied them walking across to the terrace, for she opened the door. "Well. I have just written you a note, Mr. Rattray. You saved me the trouble of sending it." She stepped aside to allow them to enter, and with a sharp glance at Lucy, invited him to tea.

"I shan't have tea, Aunt," Lucy said hastily. "I must write a letter to Papa."

Lucy scurried upstairs holding her book defensively against her chest. With a gasp, she closed the door behind her. Flinging herself on the bed, she stared up at the ceiling. Surely, her aunt didn't think Lucy had set her cap at Mr. Rattray? It would cause a great deal of trouble. She quaked at the thought.

She remained in her room until she heard the front door shut and a carriage pull away down the road.

Lucy ventured downstairs. In the morning room, her aunt sat embroidering a handkerchief.

Aunt Mary looked up. "One might think you were avoiding Mr. Rattray."

"Sitting in the sun gave me a headache."

"Would you like some feverfew?"

Lucy sank into an armchair. "No thank you, Aunt. It has gone now."

Her aunt's gaze lifted from her needlework. "Did Mr. Rattray do, or say, anything to upset you?"

"No. He is ever the gentleman."

Aunt Mary's tight shoulders appeared to ease. "He is to join us at the Williams' affair."

"He seems to enjoy your company, Aunt Mary," Lucy said carefully.

Her aunt nodded thoughtfully. "Yes. I thought so." Her gaze flickered back to Lucy's face. "But I am not as young as I was when I met your Uncle Peter."

As Lucy had nothing to say to this, she greeted Jane with relief when she walked into the room, and the conversation soon turned to books and the latest gossip.

Jane accompanied Lucy up to her bedchamber with an offer to advise her on what she might wear to the Williams' card party.

Lucy thought it strange, because Jane, while she enjoyed the freedom to choose what suited her, wasn't nearly as interested in ladies' fashion as Anabel.

When the door had shut behind them, Jane plopped down on the bed. "This bedchamber reminds me of all the painful problems I had growing up within these walls," she said. "Marriage is so much nicer."

"If you are happily married," Lucy said, taking her white muslin with the lilac ribbons and another with primrose embroidery from the wardrobe and holding them up for Jane's inspection.

"Wear the muslin with the primrose embroidery," Jane said. "Mm. I doubt Anabel is happy. She says her husband is angry because she hasn't given him an heir. And there's gossip that he has taken a mistress."

"Oh, I hope not. How awful."

"It is common practice among gentlemen who enter arranged marriages," Jane said.

"I will only marry for love," Lucy said with fierce determination.

Jane tilted her head and smiled. "Love doesn't always go so smoothly. How many can claim they found the one they love more than anyone else?"

"And I suppose finding that special love doesn't guarantee a happy future together," Lucy added glumly.

Jane turned to look at her. "Quite so," she said after a pause.

It made Lucy wonder if Jane loved her husband, because her marriage had been arranged as well. Could one have a happy marriage without love? She didn't think she could.

THE GUESTS PLAYED cards at the tables set up in the Williams' drawing room. The weather was unseasonably warm and in the confined space, the heat rivaled any ballroom Hugh had been in. Ladies put down their cards to fan their hot faces, while footmen moved among the tables serving cool drinks and wine.

Sarah played whist, while Hugh sat in on a game of faro. He was placing a card down when Mrs. Grayswood entered with Miss Kershaw and two other young ladies. The brunette was exceptionally tall.

Miss Kershaw saw him and nodded. Her aunt murmured something to her, which made her frown and shake her head.

Prompted to make a play, Hugh examined his hand. When he looked up again, Miss Kershaw had disappeared, while the three women had settled at the various tables.

As soon as the game had ended, Hugh rose and went in search of her. He found her trailing along the shelves in the musty, book-filled library.

"What are you doing here by yourself?" he asked as he entered the room. A thought struck him. Had he intruded on her awaiting someone for a clandestine meeting? The possibility of a rival and his dismay made him draw breath.

She turned to him, aghast. "Oh, Lord Dorchester. Why have you come here?"

A smile tugged at his lips. "Is the library barred to gentlemen?"

"That's nonsense," she said, her smile strained. "Do be serious, my lord. Someone might have seen you. They might think that you...and I..."

"That you and I might actually talk alone together? Something has upset you. Won't you tell me what it is?"

She gasped. "Nothing is wrong. I don't have any idea what you mean. I know you understand, my lord. You are being deliberately obtuse."

"Come, Miss Kershaw, you are the one who is obtuse for pretending nothing is wrong when I can clearly see it is? What is this all about? You can trust me."

"I needed to leave the card room before…" She shrugged and turned away. "And you've just made it worse."

He came closer and took her hands. "How so?"

She pulled her hands away. "You should not have followed me. I was trying not to stir interest in our friendship."

"Oh, is that what we are? Friends?"

"I did hope so," she said. "But I don't want everyone to learn of it."

"Because…?"

"Because…" She waved her hand. "I won't have you drawn into my problems."

"You think I can't manage anything that comes my way? You are wrong, Miss Kershaw."

"Perhaps. But why make it worse? My aunt asked me to introduce my cousins to you. While I am happy to oblige her, I wasn't about to interrupt you while you were playing faro and make a spectacle of it, so I waited until…" She shrugged.

"Until…?" he urged, a smile pulling at his lips.

"Until the proper time. If there ever is one. Aunt Mary can be very determined and was likely to insist, so… I fled." She looked so guilty that he suffered an urgent need to pull her to him.

"An introduction would have been perfectly acceptable, Miss Kershaw. You worry far too much." He took a step closer.

"Mrs. Vellacott was at the whist table," she hurriedly confessed.

"Ah, Mrs. Vellacott. But what could she possibly do?"

She raised her chin, her eyes bleak. "I am very much aware of my circumstances, my lord. The next thing we know, there will be rumors spread about us." She waved her hand as if to send him away. "Please leave. We simply must *not* be found here alone." She glanced at the door. "If someone should come in …"

"There are plenty of chaperones wandering the hallway outside. Shall I open the door?" He gestured to a chair. He wanted to stay here with her for at least a few moments more.

She folded her arms and shook her head. "It would be enough to set tongues wagging, as you are well aware."

"Are you scolding me, Miss Kershaw?"

"If I must, my lord."

He laughed. Her white, muslin gown trimmed in yellow satin with the flattering scoop neck was all the embellishment she needed. His fingers itched to tug her hair loose from a fetching topknot and see the arrangement fall onto her shoulders in a cascade of blonde curls. To breathe in her perfume. He remained where he was, lest he give in to the temptation. Or kissed her. Yes, he'd definitely kiss her.

She must have read his thoughts, for she edged around him and walked to the door. "If you won't leave, then I must."

He laughed. "Then I shall leave first. Ordered out like a young jackanapes. Will you promise to introduce me to your cousins?"

"I shall be honored." Her sweet smile would make the statue of Decebalus sigh.

"You will like Cousin Jane," she said as he went to the door.

"I look forward to it. I'll go out first. No one must see us together. You wait a while to come out after." He grinned. "We are like a pair of spies in a secret assignation, are we not?"

She laughed. "You are teasing me."

"Never."

How much he wanted to. To make her laugh and look at him that way. *The devil!* Hugh seemed unable to help himself where Miss Kershaw was concerned. He left the room slightly chastened. What was he thinking? Surely not that Miss Kershaw would be open to an arrangement? He could not play fast and loose with her reputation. What people might say about him did not matter nearly so much. Anyway, tomorrow he planned to drive down to Kent to see Miss Ashton. Perhaps he would return to London unattached. A state thus far unknown to him. Should he be… what, then? He must control these rampant emotions. He was not free yet and might never be.

As he entered the drawing room, he wondered if Sarah had noticed him leaving in Miss Kershaw's wake. If so, he'd never hear the end of it.

His fears were proved right. His sister watched him with a wry expression. Fortunately, Miss Kershaw took her time before returning. He was seated at a faro table betrothed in play, and she still hadn't come through the door. It might be enough to avoid scrutiny from the guests but would not save him from Sarah. And he could hardly deny anything she accused him of, which made it even more galling.

He sighed. A soldier's life was far less complicated than living within the dictates of society.

"Your turn, sir," the gentleman across the table prompted him.

"I beg your pardon." Hugh forced himself to concentrate on the game. Tomorrow, he must face Miss Ashton, and possibly her parents. And he wondered uneasily what might await him.

Chapter Eight

AFTER WAITING FOR ten minutes, Lucy followed Lord Dorchester to the drawing room. Lucy's fears rushed back when she met Mrs. Vellacott's critical gaze from the whist table.

When Lord Dorchester had left her alone in the library, it had helped Lucy think more clearly. She had to keep a discreet distance from him while gossip was spreading about her. Yet it became more difficult when Lady Sarah greeted her with a wave from across the room.

Aunt Mary left her seat and approached Lucy, with Jane and Anabel following closely. "Lucy, where have you been?"

"I felt in need of fresh air, aunt."

A frown deepened the fine lines on her forehead. "What nonsense."

"It is very stuffy in here, Mama," Jane said with a sympathetic glance at Lucy.

Lady Sarah's approach gave Lucy a chance to resolve her problem. "Lady Sarah, how good to see you," she said, going to greet her.

"I hoped to find you here, Miss Kershaw," Lady Sarah said, with an encompassing smile as she took in her aunt and cousins.

Lucy introduced them.

"You must meet my brother." Lady Sarah motioned towards Lord Dorchester, who had abandoned the card table to engage in conversation with another man.

He pardoned himself and came to join them.

Lady Sarah introduced everyone to him, while Lucy covertly observed Mrs. Vellacott's stony expression. Surely, the woman could make nothing of this.

Lucy could see by the smiles that Aunt Mary and her cousins were affected by Lord Dorchester's easy charm, as any lady would be. When they took their seats at the tables again, Lady Sarah took Lucy aside once Lord Dorchester had resumed his conversation with the gentleman, and Aunt Mary and her cousins returned to the tables. "Mr. Beaufort is in attendance tonight. He has completed his game. Don't turn around," she urged with a giggle. "I should like to talk to him, but I can't go over boldly and address him. Shall we take a turn about the room?"

Lucy smiled and nodded, wondering why Lady Sarah didn't ask her brother.

"I would ask Hugh," Lady Sarah said, supplying the answer as she slipped her arm into Lucy's. "But he would learn of my interest in his friend."

"And you don't want him to?"

"No. You never give brothers the upper hand, Miss Kershaw."

"I've had no experience with brothers. Since I've had none."

Lady Sarah smiled and led the way. "No, of course, you haven't. They believe it is their duty to oversee everything their younger siblings do, and I have no intention of giving in to him."

Lucy tried not to grin while thinking of Lord Dorchester in a new light. "I've noticed that men always seem to think they know better. Even though they aren't always correct."

"No, and they almost never admit it."

While conversing, they strolled across the length of the room and came upon Mr. Beaufort. Lucy found him remarkably attractive in his evening attire, with his blue eyes and black hair. And he seemed such a nice person, although rather reserved. As if he guarded his heart.

"Good evening, Mr. Beaufort," Lady Sarah said warmly. "I trust luck is with you tonight?"

He bowed. "Now that I am in the presence of two lovely ladies, it will surely improve."

"Miss Kershaw and I plan another ride in Rotten Row," Lady Sarah said surprising Lucy. "Perhaps you might join us?"

He took a step closer to Sarah. "I should be delighted." He gazed at her fondly. "Am I correct in assuming your brother is to be part of the invitation?"

"But of course." Lady Sarah looked up at him, perhaps a little distracted by his closeness. "Upon his return from the country. He leaves tomorrow."

Lucy hid her surprise, as the dowager countess was still in London. Perhaps Lord Dorchester would visit his betrothed while in Kent.

Mr. Rattray's entrance prompted her to groan under her breath. He stood for a moment, casting his eye around the room. His thoughtful gaze rested on her, and he nodded before Aunt Mary approached him.

Mr. Beaufort had been called to a table, and Lady Sarah returned to join her, having obviously enjoyed talking to him, for her eyes sparkled.

They continued their stroll. "I don't trust that gentleman," Lucy said, needing to express her doubts to someone.

"Who?" Lady Sarah looked past her.

"Mr. Rattray. The gentleman with my aunt. Do you know him?"

Lady Sarah glanced casually in their direction. "No. I don't. Perhaps Hugh does." She took Lucy's arm. "It's hot and stuffy in here. Fresh air would be welcome. Shall we go out onto the terrace?"

Lucy eagerly agreed. The night seemed filled with complications.

They donned their wraps and stood by the rail, delighting in the sight of a sliver of moon amidst a cloudless sky adorned with stars. Rose bushes scented the air, and a faint breeze lifted the leaves in the trees. The scene was ripe for romance, and Lucy yearned to be alone with Lord Dorchester again. She silently scolded herself.

Lady Sarah turned to her. "Now, tell me why you don't like Mr. Rattray."

"I'm not sure. Doesn't that make me sound mean? He has set his sights on pursuing my aunt. It's possible that he wants to marry her. It's an innate sense, but I feel something off about him, something… false… perhaps even sinister." Lucy shrugged. "It's possible that I am being fanciful."

"Women are gifted with instinct," Lady Sarah said. "You should trust it."

Lucy had to agree. "It's rarely failed me in the past."

"Mr. Beaufort is handsome, isn't he?" Lady Sarah said in a warm voice. "I had hoped… but he has shown little interest in me."

Lucy put a hand on her friend's arm. "I would give him time. I believe him to be a careful, very proper man. One who has suffered a terrible loss. And after all, your brother is his friend."

Lady Sarah's eyes widened. "Yes, he has been through a lot. You are right, as usual."

A brown-haired gentleman, appearing young and slim in comparison with Mr. Beaufort, stepped through the terrace door.

"Here you are, Lady Sarah."

"Lord Cardew, I wasn't aware that you planned to come to London." Lady Sarah crossed the terrace to him. He took her hands and gazed warmly down at her.

"It was on impulse. Mama wanted to visit a sick friend in Mayfair and wished for me to accompany her. A friend informed me he saw you riding in Hyde Park with a lady and two gentlemen. I went to your home and learned of your direction, so here I am."

"Oh, please excuse my poor manners, Lord Cardew, may I introduce you to Miss Kershaw?" Lady Sarah sounded flustered.

"Lord Cardew hails from Bath." She turned back to him. "Miss Kershaw also lives there."

Lucy bobbed. "How do you do?"

His hazel eyes roamed her face as if trying to place her. "I don't believe we've met," he said finally. "Strange, when Bath is such a small society."

"No, my lord, we have not."

"Wait," Lord Cardew said, sounding a few degrees warmer. "I recall having heard your name mentioned, Miss Kershaw. The Marquess of Berwick is a family connection, is he not?"

Horrorstruck, Lucy's heart banged in her chest. She fought to calm herself. "A distant relative, my lord." She wondered where he had heard the rumor. Was it even more widespread than she thought? She glanced back at Mrs. Vellacott, who watched her over her hand of cards.

Dismissing her, Lord Cardew turned back to Lady Sarah. "I was surprised to hear you were riding, Sarah. It's not a favorite sport of yours. Who accompanied you?"

"Miss Kershaw, Hugh, and Mr. Beaufort, a friend of my brother's."

"Beaufort? Don't know him." He gazed into the drawing room. "Is he here?"

"Yes. The gentleman standing watching play at the whist table."

"Ah." He studied Beaufort for a moment.

Lord Dorchester joined them on the terrace. "I'm surprised to find you in London, Cardew. Knowing how much you prefer Bath society."

Lord Cardew bowed. "Lord Dorchester. Mama is here to visit a friend," he said coolly.

His lordship nodded. "I see. And shall you be here long?"

"No. We return to Bath within a few days," Lord Cardew said. "My mother has obligations to fulfill in Bath."

"Of course."

Lord Dorchester's reply seemed crisp. It made Lucy wonder if he liked the gentleman. It appeared Lord Cardew was also wary of Lord Dorchester.

A strained silence followed, which Lady Sarah hurried to fill. "Shall we go in and find somewhere to sit?" she suggested, her cheeks flushed. "Unless someone intends to join a table?"

"I came to see you." Lord Cardew's hand on her arm ushered her toward the drawing room in a proprietary manner. "I can play cards anytime."

Lord Dorchester watched them cross the room and disappear into the dining room next door, where supper was served. When he glanced at Lucy, he appeared troubled. "Miss Kershaw, stay awhile?"

Her pulse galloped while her head told her sternly to refuse. "Perhaps I should…"

"We are in full view of the room, and we have been introduced."

"But Mrs. Vellacott is here tonight," she admitted, casting a discreet glance through the glass doors to where the woman played cards. "And the lady watches us now from her seat."

"Confound the woman! Ah, so that is what this is about. She will see nothing worthy of gossip here, and there's something I wish to discuss with you while Sarah is absent."

She widened her eyes. "Certainly, my lord."

He glanced at the brazier, its flames attracting insects. "I must travel to the country tomorrow. You seem eminently sensible, Miss Kershaw," he said, turning back to her, his eyes taking in every feature of her face. "I'd be grateful, if Sarah should seek your advice, that you would dissuade her from being swayed by anything Lord Cardew might suggest."

"I doubt it will occur. I am not a confidante of Lady Sarah's, and I know Lord Cardew not at all," Lucy said firmly. "I cannot imagine she would listen to anything I might have to say."

His eyes searched hers. "My sister is not foolish. Please understand. But she has one weakness, and that is Lord Cardew. He might consider the time right while I am away from London to lead Sarah astray, and I've no doubt he will act on it. I don't believe he has Sarah's best interests at heart. Should you feel Sarah is about to make a mistake, if you could please try to counsel her, I'd be grateful."

"I would love to help, my lord. But I am hardly in a position to counsel anyone. I have made mistakes of my own, of which you are very well aware."

He laughed softly, his gaze resting for a moment on her mouth. "What a disgraceful woman you must be, Miss Kershaw."

Lucy smiled. Oh, why did he look at her like that? They were on display before the whole drawing room. She tried so hard to keep away from him, while he drew her like those moths around the brazier fire. She felt herself wishing for the impossible. "Rest assured, Lord Dorchester, if I am in a position to offer advice to Lady Sarah and feel it would be helpful, I shall do so, although I can't imagine anything to occur to warrant it."

He straightened. "That is all I ask, Miss Kershaw. Shall we go inside? I believe supper is being served in the dining room."

When Lucy took his proffered arm, emotion rushed through her so strong, she missed a step.

"Steady there." He looked down at her, a world of meaning in his eyes. "I've got you."

Perhaps in her dreams, she thought, wryly trying to pull herself together as they passed through the door.

HUGH DROVE HIS town carriage east toward the rising sun. Departing London at cock's crow, he planned to spend as little time as possible in Kent. He wasn't sure his mother could handle Sarah, even supposing Sarah took her into her confidence. She might confide in Miss Kershaw, however. Could he trust Cardew? The man had narrowed his eyes when he looked at Luke, as if sizing him up as a rival. There was no misinterpreting his possessive manner toward Sarah. If he'd done what had been expected of him several years ago, he might have that right. But as it was, he must stand in line with other suitors who showed an interest in his sister. How he would handle that was something Hugh couldn't guess at. But Cardew lacked maturity. He was spoiled and remained under his mother's thumb. Nor was Hugh sure of Sarah. She was obviously still fond of the man. Hugh had hoped her attention might be drawn to Luke Beaufort, but so far, it hadn't blossomed into a romance.

Hugh drove into the stable courtyard at Woodcroft in the afternoon. Entering the house, he greeted his butler and arranged to see his secretary, estate manager, and bailiff the following day, then went up to change.

He rode his horse, Chance, along the road to his neighbors' estate. When he arrived, the day was drawing to a close, and as he'd skipped luncheon, he hoped to be invited to dinner. He had known the Ashton family since he'd been a boy. His father had been a staunch friend of Sir Phillip's.

Hugh was shown into the drawing room. "Lord Dorchester, good to see you." Sir Phillip, a very tall gentleman whose head almost brushed the door lintel, came to shake his hand. His stance was upright stance his jaw strong. "How is your mother?"

Lady Ashton remained seated.

"Good to see you, Sir Phillip, Lady Ashton. Mother is in need of rest. I hope to persuade her to come home soon, but as Sarah is enjoying the Season, it proves difficult." Hugh shook his hand, thinking new lines of strain marked Isabel's father's face. Lady Ashton, a small, bird-like woman, was also in some distress, her eyes swollen and red from crying. Hugh crossed the carpet to greet her where she sat rigidly in an armchair. She offered her hand, a damp handkerchief clutched in the other. Her eyes were red, and she actually glowered at him. Hugh was taken aback. What was this?

"I came hoping to see Miss Ashton," he said, feeling the need to explain.

"We have news," Sir Phillip said, standing with legs apart in front of the fireplace. "Unpleasant as it is, you must be informed of it."

"What is it?" Hugh asked, frowning slightly. Not an illness?

Her mother dabbed at her eyes with the lace-edged square. "Isabel is unwell."

"She is not unwell," Sir Phillip said. "Confound it, Marion. Isabel is with child."

There was a stunned silence while Hugh struggled to find the appropriate response.

"The father is Benson, our vicar," her father said plainly outraged. "The bloody *vicar!*"

"Hush, Gerald," Lady Ashton said in a faint tone. "The servants will hear. If only you hadn't gone off to war, Lord Dorchester." She continued to glare accusingly at him. "And left Isabel for years! You barely know each other."

Hugh thought it remarkable that she expected him to have spent a good deal of his time with a girl not yet out, but she was so upset, he didn't attempt to counter her argument. Lady Ashton put a hand to her pale cheek. "You might be married now." She gazed at him hopefully. "Perhaps you might still…"

"No, Marian," her husband thundered. "Allow him to deal with this as he sees fit."

"What does Miss Ashton want to do?" Hugh asked.

Sir Phillip shrugged. "Who knows? She has some convoluted notion that makes no sense at all."

"Miss Ashton is here? May I see her?"

"But of course, Lord Dorchester." Lady Ashton straightened her back, sniffed and dried her eyes. "You'll find Isabel in the conservatory."

Hugh strode down the hall, wondering what Miss Ashton might say to him. Would she want him to marry her? Whatever her mother said, and despite her being in the schoolroom while he'd been at university, they had been friends. He'd taught her to fish for trout in the river. Miss Ashton had once unsuccessfully tried to teach him to crochet with a great deal of laughter. If she needed him, he would marry her and claim the child as his. But the thought made him bitter.

He found her examining a pot of pink cyclamens, a trowel in her hand. When she saw him, she gave a start and her face paled. "You've heard?"

"Yes." He came to kiss her cool cheek.

She placed a hand lightly on his shoulder, holding herself stiffly.

"Do you wish to marry me, Miss Ashton… Isabel?"

She shook her head. "What sort of marriage would we have? Even if you are the generous man I think you are, I would make a terrible wife and the babe will not be yours. I won't do that to you. No doubt Mama hopes we might still marry. But it will not happen."

"What about Mr. Benson?" He frowned. "Why isn't he here to support you?"

"Michael had to attend the village fete," she said. "He has discussed our future with my parents."

Hugh would have liked to hear that conversation. "So that makes this all right?"

She looked defensive. "He is the third son of a wealthy, titled family."

"I wonder more about his beliefs." Hugh knew not all vicars were especially religious, but one expected them to be upstanding members of the community.

"I know what you're thinking. But it was all my doing." She shrugged. "We love each other. Michael has told them he is prepared to take a parish somewhere in England if we marry. But I don't want to remain here. It wouldn't matter where we went in this country. Rumors spread. It would be too hard on Mama."

"But where would you go?"

"Michael has had a living offered him in Ceylon," she said, motioning Hugh to a pair of wicker chairs. "He requires a wife." Her lips firmed. "I shall go with him."

Hugh stared at her as they took their seats. "That would be difficult, Isabel, even dangerous."

"I'm aware of that."

"It would be a very harsh life. You have not been brought up to face such hardship."

"Nevertheless, I intend to go. It is for the best. Papa feels my disgrace will ruin the family name and standing in the community. While Mama still yearns to see me married to you and living nearby."

"Is there anything I can do?"

She shook her head. "Thank you, but no. Because I was yet to make my debut, our betrothal was never formally announced. It's my hope that gossip and speculation will die down quickly after I leave England. Father will come up with some acceptable reason for my absence." She reached across and took his hand, squeezing it, her eyes gentle. "You are free to marry someone you love, Hugh. Be happy."

"We could have made a go of marriage, Isabel," he said. "Your mother seems to feel I failed you when I joined the army."

"What nonsense. We were only ever friends. This is entirely my fault. I want more from life than an arranged marriage, and so do you."

He had to admit it was true. While he feared for Isabel's future, he realized how strong she was, mentally at least. But physically? "Is the vicar a good man?" He clamped his jaw at the urge to draw the man's cork.

"Indeed, he is."

"I'll visit him and ensure he has your interest at heart."

She placed a hand on his arm. "No, Hugh. Michael was quite prepared to remain here. He put no pressure on me. It was I who refused. This is the work he has always yearned for, and he is passionate about it. I want to help him. To be by his side through thick and thin."

"But will you leave before the baby is born? The sea voyage…"

"I shall endure it. I sent you a letter, explaining all this, but you obviously haven't yet received it. Michael has arranged for the vicar of St. Martin's in Canterbury to marry us in a month's time after the banns are read. We'll sail the following day." She looked so different, so animated, her eyes gleaming, her cheeks flushed. "I am looking forward to the trip. To visit a new, exotic land. To have the Lord's work to do. Never have I felt this excited and hopeful. And you must know I would have made a very bad countess."

"I doubt that." He sighed, concern for her tightening his chest. "Will you write?"

Isabel nodded with a smile. "Of course." She bent forward, put a hand on his shoulder, and kissed his cheek.

Hugh declined to dine with the Ashtons. Isabel's determination to depart England in a few weeks had brought on a fresh set of tears and moans from her mother. Her father glowered, a line of white around his hard-clenched mouth.

"We need to keep this secret until Isabel leaves the country," he said to Hugh. "There were many expecting you two to marry. Can I ask that of you, Lord Dorchester?"

"But of course, sir."

Hugh thought he was intruding and that he no longer had any place there. As he rode home, he felt as if a chunk of his life had been ripped away. But at the same time, the sudden release of tension in his body that he'd hardly been aware of, made him gasp. After supper, he sat in the library with a book on his knee he barely glanced at. It suddenly hit him. In a month, he was free to choose his partner in life. Acknowledging it made him lightheaded. He'd never realized how much his and Isabel's arranged marriage had weighed on him. And shaped his life.

The clock struck midnight when he finally climbed the stairs. With his batman-come-valet, Wickstaff, visiting his sick mother, Hugh prepared for bed and slipped beneath the covers. Blowing out the candle, he lay in the dark, his mind too busy for sleep. He had not wanted to marry Isabel, in truth. But for it to end this way...

With a deep sigh, he decided to visit Mr. Benson tomorrow and make sure the vicar was everything Isabel thought him. But if Hugh was unconvinced of the man's ability to take care of her, what could he do? She was so determined, he doubted she'd listen to reason. And the truth was that her life as she knew it would be finished should she remain in England. Unless a suitable husband was quickly found. It didn't stop the anger boiling inside him. The vicar didn't deserve her. What does a tenderly raised girl know of life at eighteen? To seduce her before marriage, and whatever Isabel said to the contrary, he should have taken control of the situation to protect her. It will be difficult to face the man when Hugh itched to give him a good thrashing.

Giving vent physically to his anger was impossible. It would only make matters worse. After he'd seen his staff in the morning, he'd stop at the presbytery on his way up to London. He was anxious to be back in the city. He didn't trust Cardew, who seemed put out by a possible rival. Might the man now be considering marrying Sarah? Hugh very much doubted Cardew would go against his mother's wishes. Yet Hugh didn't trust him an inch. As Sarah's older brother and guardian, he could insist she never spoke to Cardew again. But he knew her too well. It would only serve to make her rebel.

He allowed his thoughts to dwell on Miss Kershaw. Would he see her again soon? She was as skittish as a foal, determined to remain aloof from him because of some misplaced idea that she would draw him into a scandal. But he had to admit there was reason for her concern. Word had obviously spread about her supposed inheritance, thanks, he supposed, to Mrs. Vellacott. He had noticed the woman's sour expression as she'd sat at the table at the Williams' party. She might believe the rumor to be true and was gaining some notoriety for herself by being the first to share the news, but his gut feeling told him she knew it was a lie and had taken it upon herself to spread that nasty rumor, keen to discover more fuel to add to the fire. Though the reason why it concerned her so much, he couldn't imagine. Was it merely the loss of a few pounds in a bad investment?

Chapter Nine

WHILE LUCY SORTED through her clothes in her bedchamber, a maid knocked to inform her Lady Sarah waited below to see her.

Lucy entered the drawing room, where Lady Sarah, dressed in her riding habit, tapped her crop against her skirts as she stood before the fireplace. She turned and pressed her hands to her chest. "Miss Kershaw, I am so pleased to have found you at home."

"How nice to see you, Lady Sarah. Will you stay for tea?"

Lady Sarah shook her head firmly. "No, there's no time to. I need your help. Now, if that's possible."

"I'm happy to be of assistance, if you'll just tell me what—"

"I'm sorry that this is dreadfully rushed," Lady Sarah rushed to explain. "But if you have nothing planned for this morning, will you join me for a ride in the park?"

Surprised, and a little alarmed by Lady Sarah's manner, Lucy sought for a way to calm her and get to the bottom of her anxiety. "Certainly, if you wish me to. But please sit for a moment."

Lady Sarah perched on the edge of the sofa, her eyes restlessly viewing the room. "Lord Cardew has written. He wishes to see me in Hyde Park today. Alone."

Lucy sat beside her. "Did he say why?"

"No, but Hugh will be so cross with me if I go by myself. That's why I need you to accompany me."

"I am happy to, but won't Lord Cardew be annoyed to find me with you?"

"Perhaps." She gripped her hands together. "It doesn't matter. I need you. Will you come?"

"Of course I will."

Lady Sarah jumped up. "Thank you, Miss Kershaw. I knew you wouldn't let me down. I cannot tell Mama about this, and I can't trust my maid. She is sure to give in to questioning. Mama is suffering from yet another headache. I'll wait while you change into your habit. My groom will accompany us."

When Lucy told Aunt Mary, her aunt smiled and nodded. "You are becoming bosom friends with Lady Sarah."

Lucy thought about her aunt's assumption while Maisie helped her dress for riding. She liked to think it was true.

As their horses trotted down Rotten Row, the groom trailing well behind, Lord Cardew rode out of the trees, a scowl on his face. He drew his horse close to Sarah's. "I asked you to come alone, Sarah."

"That would not have been wise," Lady Sarah said. "What is it you wish to talk to me about, Lord Cardew?"

"Come a little way into the park with me. Miss Kershaw will wait here with the groom. Won't you, Miss Kershaw?"

"I will do what Lady Sarah wishes," Lucy said, determined not to be browbeaten.

Lady Sarah's smile was strained. She ordered the groom to stay with Lucy. "I'll only be a few minutes, Miss Kershaw. We won't venture far."

While she waited, Lucy rode her horse slowly down the Row, then back to the spot where Lady Sarah had disappeared with Lord Cardew. About fifteen minutes had passed, and then that stretched to twenty. The groom approached her, looking anxious.

"What should we do, Miss Kershaw? It's more than my life is worth to go home without Lady Sarah."

"I'm sure that won't be the case. She is with a gentleman of long standing." Lucy peered anxiously into the park. "But we must keep this to ourselves," she said, gazing sternly at the groom.

Another five minutes passed. Lord Dorchester had asked her to look out for Lady Sarah. It had seemed strange at the time, but now she understood. While considering what to do next, three men cantered down the Row. One of them broke away and rode over to her. Mr. Beaufort raised his hat. "Miss Kershaw. You seem to be alone. Is anything wrong?"

Lucy took a moment to think. Should she involve him in this? She was in a quandary. But she had no option. "I am waiting for Lady Sarah. She rode into the park with Lord Cardew and was only to be gone for a few minutes. But it's now closer to half an hour."

He stared at her, concern in his eyes. "Which way did they go?"

"They rode through there." She pointed with her crop to the break in the trees.

"Then let's go and find them, shall we?" He turned back to the groom. "Wait here, please."

"Why not bring the groom?" Lucy asked him as they rode away from Rotten Row.

"We don't want any gossip to be spread about. And servants tend to talk."

What did he expect to find? Still questioning the wisdom of going after them, Lucy rode with him through the trees and onto the parkland. She could find no sign of Lady Sarah or Lord Cardew.

They continued their search for several minutes, following a well-worn path through the grass. In the daisy-strewn meadow, two horses grazed, their reins looped over bushes.

They heard voices from somewhere behind a thicket of dense shrubs. Their words were impossible to make out, but the man's voice was cajoling, and the lady's appeared to be entreating.

Mr. Beaufort glanced at Lucy, his eyebrows raised, and urged his horse on. He rounded the trees, with Lucy riding close behind.

Lady Sarah stood against the trunk of a majestic chestnut tree. Lord Cardew leaned over her, a hand resting on the trunk above her head. The other at her waist. Lucy could see she was upset.

Mr. Beaufort dismounted. When the two failed to see him, he coughed.

Lord Cardew spun around. "What on Earth...?" His weak, indulgent features pulled into a scowl. "Do you not respect a person's privacy, sir?"

Beaufort calmly walked over to him. "My concern is with the lady."

Lady Sarah pushed away from Lord Cardew and rushed over to Lucy, where she sat on her horse. "I'm sorry you had to wait so long," she said, appearing shaky, yet determined to keep some modicum of good manners.

"I hope you don't mind me coming," Lucy said. "I had to know if you were all right. I confess to growing a little worried."

Mr. Beaufort led Lady Sarah's mare to her. "May I help you mount, my lady?"

Lady Sarah blushed vividly. "Thank you, sir."

Lord Cardew went to his horse. Mounted, he turned back to stare at Lady Sarah. When she made no move to speak to him, barely acknowledging him, he galloped away.

Watching Lord Cardew disappear among the trees, Lady Sarah murmured her thanks to Mr. Beaufort. She looked at Lucy, her blue eyes shadowed. "Let's return home."

Mr. Beaufort accompanied them back to Rotten Row, where the groom waited. When Lady Sarah attempted to thank her rescuer again, he shook his head. "I did nothing that warrants your thanks, Lady Sarah. I suspect it was Miss Kershaw's fierce stare that sent the gentleman on his way."

Lady Sarah smiled, and Lucy couldn't help grinning.

He lifted his hat, then rode away to join his friends.

"I hope I did the right thing coming to find you," Lucy said again, aware that Lady Sarah had suffered some embarrassment. "I thought you looked uncomfortable with Lord Cardew."

"I must explain," Lady Sarah said, her voice trembling.

"Not if you don't wish it."

"Lord Cardew is an old friend. Robert promised to marry me on a number of occasions over the last two years, but there was always something to prevent it. I waited because I loved him and would have accepted him, despite Hugh's disapproval of him." She shook her head sadly. "But that is no longer of any importance."

Lucy gazed at her with concern as two ladies trotted down the row with their grooms.

Seeing the women, Lady Sarah turned her horse toward the stables. They rode on for several minutes before she spoke. "Robert said he loved me. He doesn't want to give me up," she said, sounding bitter.

"Well, that must be a good thing, must it not?"

"No, it isn't. He is about to become betrothed to Lady Gwendolyn, the Duke of Kendal's daughter."

Lucy's heart ached. She turned in the saddle to observe her miserable friend. "Then I believe you have had a fortunate escape," she said gently.

Lady Sarah raised her eyebrows. "You think so?"

"I do." Lucy believed Lord Cardew was jealous. He'd looked furious when he saw Mr. Beaufort at the card party, and again today. "Did he propose marriage again?"

Sarah slowly shook her head.

"Nor did he say he would approach your brother and ask for your hand. His declaration of love was insulting. What was his intention? You can do far better than Lord Cardew."

Lady Sarah nodded but frowned and bit her lip.

Did she still hope Lord Cardew would marry her? It seemed most unlikely now when he was about to become betrothed.

It made Lucy think of Lord Dorchester and the powerful attraction they shared. He was also betrothed. What might he want of her? She must remain strong, although she feared she was weak where he was concerned.

"You are right, Miss Kershaw," Lady Sarah said, after a moment. She sighed. "Mr. Beaufort behaved in an exemplary manner, did he not?"

"He is a true gentleman," Lucy said. "I find I like him a great deal."

"I do too," Lady Sarah admitted. "But what must he think of me?"

"He would have been pleased to have helped you when an unscrupulous man tried to manipulate you for his own gain."

Lady Sarah glanced at her and nodded. "Please don't tell Hugh about this. My brother will be so angry with him. I fear he will want to teach Lord Cardew a lesson."

"No, of course I won't mention it."

They rode into the stable courtyard. "I am delighted to have you as my friend, Miss Kershaw," Lady Sarah said as the groom hurried over to help them dismount.

"And I am glad we are friends. Do call me 'Lucy,' Lady Sarah."

She smiled. "Lucy, please call me 'Sarah.'"

Hugh sat beside his mother as she rested on the sofa in the morning room. A shaft of sunlight fell upon her shawl, brightening its warm colors, making her look even paler. He felt a rush of concern.

Hugh had arrived in London late last evening when everyone had been abed. Earlier, he'd spent over an hour talking to the vicar at the vicarage before leaving Kent. He was a good-looking man in a slender, poetical kind of way. Benson had seemed uncomfortable to be talking to the man Isabel had been meant to marry. He had taken great pains to assure Hugh that he would take precious care of her. But Hugh thought he didn't look robust enough to withstand the rigors of such a position. He seemed out of his depth. The vicar might believe in his words, but actually being able to keep Isabel safe in a foreign country with a babe would prove extremely difficult. And he wasn't even sure Benson was as confident as Isabel appeared to be.

Benson had made no attempt to explain his actions or ask forgiveness for them, leaving Hugh to suspect Isabel had been the force behind it, as she had admitted. But a man in Benson's situation should have been above such things. Furious with him for his lack of self-control, Hugh had been tempted to quote from the Bible: *The Lord Jesus taught His disciples to ask God, "And do not lead us into temptation, but deliver us from evil."* If someone asked God to help others avoid temptation, then that person should also stay away from tempting situations.

Trouble was, should he mention it, Hugh would be a hypocrite. He was only too familiar with how powerful temptation could be. He had come away thinking Benson would not want to hurt Isabel for the world, but it was foolish to believe the vicar could keep her safe.

Hugh had given his promise to Sir Phillip and Lady Ashton, who were struggling with the imminent loss of their daughter. He wouldn't be free until Isabel had married and left England.

He wished to declare his intentions to Miss Kershaw, but the whispers about the lady's father's inheritance persisted, and he could not allow the threat of scandal to fall upon his family. Not his fragile mother, and Sarah.

Hugh intended first to put a stop to this insidious gossip. He would stare down Mrs. Vellacott and her ilk as soon as he was free to marry. Then he would have to convince Miss Kershaw the gossip was at an end, or she wouldn't have him. His hands were tied for a month! Would she even be free then? He thought of the men, like Nash, who were exhibiting far too much interest in her, and tightened his jaw.

"Poor Miss Ashton," his mother said for the third time, breaking into his thoughts. "I cannot see her coping in a heathenish country."

"I've never seen her so happy," Hugh said. Although his mother looked confused, he could not tell her the real reason for their marriage.

"Foolish girl. She might have married you, Hugh."

"She chose the vicar." He shrugged. "Who can understand the mysteries of the heart?"

"Well, I am confident that you will be much more judicious in your choice of bride."

"Because her name has been linked with mine, Sir Phillip believed it best not to speak of it or to cause any speculation until Isabel has left the country." Hugh rose from the sofa. "Where is Sarah?"

"She is riding with Miss Kershaw. Sarah seems to have taken to the girl. She should be home soon. Perhaps Miss Kershaw will come with her." She eyed Hugh thoughtfully. "They say her father is the Marquess of Berwick's heir. I don't know the family, do you?"

"Not well. They live near Carlisle, close to the Scottish border, But, Mama, that is neither here nor there. You shouldn't believe everything you hear or read in the gossip sheets."

His mother narrowed her eyes slightly. "I don't read gossip sheets, Hugh. But there's seldom smoke without fire."

"I'll walk down to meet Sarah," he said, refusing to discuss it further and suffer a barrage of further questions. "Might hire a horse. It will be pleasant to ride on such a sunny day. I'll go and change into my riding clothes."

As he left the house on foot, Hugh met his sister and Miss Kershaw walking up the road from the stables with the groom.

He returned Sarah's suspiciously casual greeting, noticing twin spots of color on her cheeks and wondering what had happened during his absence.

"Lucy has agreed to join us for luncheon," Sarah said. "Did you enjoy your trip to Kent? How is Miss Ashton?"

"She is well." Hugh took note of his sister's use of Miss Kershaw's first name. They were becoming bosom friends, and while that pleased him, it would be torture to see a lot of Miss Kershaw during the next month and be unable to pursue her. "Mother will tell you more about that. After a ride, I'll see you at luncheon." He glanced casually at Miss Kershaw, noting the intense look in her eyes beneath the rim of her black riding hat. Was she sending him some kind of warning? "Did you enjoy your ride, Miss Kershaw?"

"I did. Thank you, my lord."

"Mr. Beaufort might still be in the park," Sarah said. "We saw him there with some gentlemen." She blushed. "You might invite him to luncheon."

"Very well." Hugh walked on, his crop resting on his shoulder while his mind remained on the lady who was ever present in his thoughts. Her guarded expression. Sarah's skittish mood. Had something occurred he should know about?

Hugh returned to the house over an hour later and told Sarah, as she and Miss Kershaw started up the stairs, that Beaufort was coming to luncheon after he changed out of his riding clothes. He was gratified to see how pleased Sarah was, but a romance required reciprocation, and his friend had given no hint that he was interested in Sarah.

He hoped to have a quiet word with Miss Kershaw, when she and Sarah came down from freshening up.

When Sarah excused herself to see her mother, Hugh took his chance. He stood with his back to the fire, at a distance from where Miss Kershaw sat on the drawing room sofa. "Did something untoward happen in the park this morning?"

She frowned. "I'm not at liberty to tell you."

"Dash it all, Miss Kershaw. Don't you believe it is important enough for me to know?"

She rubbed her brow. "I do, but I cannot break Sarah's confidence." Her clear gaze searched his. "You might ask her your-self."

"It appears I must."

Determined not to allow him to wrangle information from her, she raised her chin.

"As Mr. Beaufort is coming to luncheon, you might ask him about it."

"Luke was there in the park?"

"Yes, he was very helpful."

Hugh cocked an eyebrow. But she firmed her lips and refused to say more.

"Very well, I shall ask him," he said finally as Sarah entered the room.

"What are you two talking about?" She glanced from one to the other. "You look like two conspirators plotting someone's defeat."

"Like a pair of spies?" Hugh asked Sarah. He glanced at Miss Kershaw and was rewarded by a blush. "Might you have something to tell me?"

Sarah's quizzical gaze went again from his to Miss Kershaw's. "No, I don't believe so."

"As you wish." Not convinced, he nodded.

Hugh left the room and went upstairs to change. He would have better success with Luke. A man could be relied upon to reveal something he considered of vital importance. Men were far more sensible than most women, who kept their friends' secrets to the grave. Hugh chuckled. He admired Miss Kershaw's loyalty, and her hint that Luke might be at liberty to explain the situation, even though it had frustrated him.

When Luke arrived, Hugh took him aside. "Did something untoward occur in the park this morning with my sister?

Luke cleared his throat, alarm in his eyes. "She hasn't told you?"

"No."

"Lady Sarah might not approve of me telling you." After a

moment, Luke shrugged. "But I feel you should know what I witnessed, at least. Viscount Cardew was with her. The pair had left Miss Kershaw waiting on Rotten Row with the groom and ridden deeper into the park. When Miss Kershaw and I found them, Lord Cardew was holding Lady Sarah against a tree. I wasn't sure if it was a lovers' tiff, but she looked distressed, and I disliked the manner in which he treated her."

"The swine!" Hugh roared.

Luke nodded his agreement, his forehead furrowed. "When I questioned Lord Cardew as to what he was about, he didn't take it kindly and rode off." He lifted his eyebrows. "I hope what I did was in order?"

Hugh gritted his teeth. "Indeed it was. I am relieved you were there."

Hugh left Luke in the drawing room with Miss Kershaw, the footman serving them wine, and went to speak to Sarah, whom he found with their mother.

"A word, Sarah?" Hugh fought to stay calm.

"What is it, Hugh?" His mother's eyes widened.

"A small matter, Mama." He escorted his sister out of the room.

Sarah turned to him in the hall, her eyes narrowed. "Who told you?"

"Miss Kershaw remained tight-lipped, but Luke told me about Cardew drawing you away from Rotten Row and leaving Miss Kershaw to wait for you."

"Yes, I felt sure he would tell you," she said with a frown.

"He only revealed it when I asked him. He is worried about you."

She sighed. "Mr. Beaufort was a great help."

"What was Cardew's reason to behave so appallingly?" Hugh asked.

"He wished to tell me he is to marry Lady Gwendolyn Piper."

Hugh, relieved at the news, studied her face for signs of distress and was reassured not to find it. "That was all? Why the secrecy?"

She shrugged. "It doesn't matter now."

Hugh curled his fingers into his palms, believing there was much more to the story she wasn't telling him. "If he intended anything else, I'll make him very sorry."

"There's no need. Lord Cardew intends to leave for Bath tomorrow with his mother. I shan't see him again."

Hugh released a breath. He patted her cheek. "It's for the best, Sarah, love."

Her expression saddened. "Miss Kershaw thought so too. I'm sure she's right."

"Now that we are four, shall we play a game of whist after luncheon?" he said to cheer her.

She smiled and slipped an arm through his. "That would be agreeable."

They walked along the corridor to the drawing room. "Mr. Beaufort seems a very decent gentleman," Sarah said.

"He is," Hugh said, careful not to appear too eager as he opened the door and stepped back for her to pass through it.

Luke appeared more at ease during the card game. They laughed as he related a story about a ram on his property who'd taken it into its mind to herd him away from the flock. "When I turned my back, he butted me like a goat," he said, grinning. "I fell over into the mud, my dignity in shreds, causing the farmer who was with me to laugh uproariously."

Sarah giggled and clapped her hands. It heartened Hugh. He'd like to see her marry a man who was not afraid to get his hands dirty. Instead of a strutting, spoiled peacock like Cardew.

After the game finished, Sarah played "Robin Adair" on the piano and Miss Kershaw was persuaded to sing.

Once the strains of music ebbed away, everyone applauded vigorously.

"You have a lovely voice, Miss Kershaw," Luke said, and Hugh agreed, enjoying her sweet soprano, and especially how the rays of sunlight had fallen upon her golden hair.

Sarah played again while Luke sang in a strong baritone.

Hugh was pleased to see the spark of interest which passed between the performers.

"Encore!" Miss Kershaw called with a wide smile.

Flushing, Sarah shuffled the music sheets and conversed with Luke.

Hugh clapped his encouragement, but his attention was caught by Miss Kershaw and her delightful smile, warm and inviting. Emotion stirred within him, a need to grow closer, to know her completely. He'd come close to losing control once before when he'd briefly held her as he'd assisted her from the carriage, and he needed to keep his distance until Isabel was married. But what if Nash still pursued her? Her grace and beauty made it impossible for her to be overlooked, plus the rumor of her father's connections, which would be attractive to men, some respectable and some not.

It would be easier if Sarah stopped throwing Miss Kershaw in his way. Hugh suspected his sister had decided they were meant for each other. He needed to cool his heels until he was viewed as entirely free of any commitment. While he did so, he'd make inquiries about Mr. Rattray. If, as Miss Kershaw had said, the man was interested in marrying her aunt, why had he watched Miss Kershaw so closely at the card party?

Chapter Ten

A MAID WITH purple bags under her eyes accompanied them in the landau when Lord Dorchester drove Lucy back to her aunt's townhouse. It was late afternoon, and shadows stole across the lawns in Green Park.

He broke the companionable silence which had grown between them. The maid, poor woman, had fallen asleep in the seat behind them. "Luke told me what he witnessed between Sarah and Viscount Cardew in Hyde Park. I confess to being very alarmed and very angry. I've been considering whether to act on it."

"That might make matters worse." Lucy looked askance at him, fearing this could lead to violence. He might be hurt, or worse. She trembled at the thought. "And could send Sarah into his arms," she added, hoping to dissuade him.

"Mm, it might at that," he said noncommittally.

That didn't completely reassure her, but she was pleased he'd confided in her. She could offer little without breaking Sarah's confidence. "I hoped Mr. Beaufort would tell you. Lord Cardew said he's leaving for Bath within a day or so. Perhaps that will be the end of it?"

His worried gaze came to rest on her questioning eyes. "That remains to be seen. Do you think Sarah is still in danger of being influenced by him?"

"I honestly can't say. Surely, it's unlikely he will bother her again, not now he is about to become betrothed."

"It won't be easy for Sarah to accept the fellow is out of her life."

Lucy studied his handsome profile as he guided the horses along a narrow road. "It might take a while. But once she meets someone else…"

"Cardew has been a constant presence since they met years ago. Nothing was formally declared, but promises were made. He gave Sarah to understand they would marry." He frowned. "Was that all he wanted to see her about when he whisked her away from Rotten Row? Only to tell her of his betrothal? I doubt it. Why did he need to have her to himself?"

Lucy deliberated whether she should break Sarah's confidence and then decided it was unnecessary because Lord Cardew no longer appeared to be a threat. "I don't know what occurred before Mr. Beaufort and I rode up to them, so I really cannot say, my lord."

He cocked an eyebrow. "Sarah must have confided something to you about what happened between them."

"She did tell me a little of what was said. But I promised not to reveal it." She flushed, embarrassed. "You must ask her."

"Very well, Miss Kershaw." He interrupted her with a sigh. "You would make an excellent spy."

Lucy laughed. "I'm not sure how I'd react to torture."

"I'm glad you will never find out. Nothing should ever mar your perfect beauty." When his gaze settled on her mouth, she caught her breath.

She feared she was blushing. "My grandmother used to say, 'Beauty is as beauty does.'"

"Chaucer, I believe. I merely speak the truth. You are lovely in many ways, Lucy."

Her pulse raced. He had called her by her Christian name. His audacity made her smile, despite herself. He was soon to marry. But she still yearned to hear more from him—like what he admired about her, apart from her appearance. Would it be enough to cancel her terrible lie? Lucy became annoyed with herself. If only she could stop building castles in the air.

The phaeton turned onto her aunt's street, the slumbering maid so silent behind them, Lucy had almost forgotten she was there. A moment later, he pulled the horses to a stop. He sat glancing down at the reins in his hands, while she waited, biting her lip, wondering what he might say.

"I need to travel north for a few weeks on business," he said finally. "It's my hope that you will see more of Sarah in my absence." He hesitated. "I believe you are a steadying influence on her. And am I right in assuming you enjoy my sister's company?"

"I do. I have grown very fond of Sarah." But it was not her place to instigate the course of their friendship, although she didn't say so. He would be as aware of the strict conventions as she was.

"When you are with my sister, or at any other time, always take a servant or groom with you." He looked at her, his gaze drifting over her face. "And be careful who you take up with, Lucy. London can be a dangerous place for young women," he added after a moment. Then before she could question him, he turned away and jumped down from the carriage.

What did he mean? Must he be so obscure? Was it because of the young maid's presence? It hadn't seemed to bother him before. His touch was impersonal as he helped Lucy to the footpath, and nothing like before, when they'd lingered too close, growing breathless, and despite knowing he could never be hers, and how foolish she was, she still hoped he might kiss her. That at least, she'd have that memory to hold to her heart.

Without another word, he escorted her to the door.

He left her with a brief farewell, and she stood there to watch him drive away, puzzled by the change in him. Something must have transpired to alter his attitude toward her, but she had no idea what it might be. Daring to call her by her given name surprised and confused her. He must realize how impossible it was for them to be together? Hadn't she tried to keep her distance from him for his sake? She wished she could convince herself that there really was no future for her with him. Lords married into wealthy families, or noble ones. And she came from neither. She struggled to imagine what future she could see for herself with this horrid rumor hanging over her head. A rumor which threatened to grow into a scandal, which would paint her as a terrible fraud and banish her from London for all time.

Glum, Lucy walked indoors, contemplating her situation. Mr. Nash still pursued her, as well as several other gentlemen, but troubled as she was, she could not conceive of spending her life with any of them. That was because of Lord Dorchester. It was foolish to deny it.

Aunt Mary met her in the hall. "Mr. Nash called earlier and left his card. He wished to take you up in his carriage for a ride to the park."

"Did he?" Lucy struggled to ponder his reason to drive with her again so soon, her thoughts still on Lord Dorchester.

"He said he will call again tomorrow." Aunt Mary smiled. "You have become popular, Lucy. And here you were thinking you would not take to the Season."

Had Lucy thought that? Or had it been her aunt's fear? Should she still fear it? Deep in thought that night in her bedroom, Lucy heard someone knock at the door. She opened it and greeted Jane. Glad of the distraction, Lucy welcomed her cousin with a warm hug. "Shall we go down and have some tea?" she asked Jane.

"Not yet. I have something to tell you, which I don't want Mama to hear," Jane said, her eyes grave and her forehead creased with concern.

Alarmed, Lucy patted the bed beside her. "What is it?"

"Anabel told me she has taken a lover." Jane groaned and scrubbed her face with her hands. "If Mama hears of it, there will be a terrible fuss! And if Anabel's husband does, I fear for her future."

"Doesn't Anabel's husband know?"

Jane shook her head.

"Won't he suspect it?"

"As Howe's seldom at home, he might not learn of it for a while. At least not until the gossip reaches him." Jane shrugged, her eyes sad. "Or Anabel tells him. She is very cavalier about it. She said what's sauce for the goose is sauce for the gander. It's almost as if she doesn't care."

"Why would she feel that way?"

"She is doing it out of spite. To teach him a lesson."

"Oh." Lucy thought it extremely foolish of her. Men could get away with so much more. If Howe learned about his wife's infidelity, it would cause upheaval and pain for her and her family. Even divorce, as Howe was a powerful, wealthy man. "Point out to Anabel how reckless she is being. Tell her to be discreet. If she continues with this, and Howe discovers he is cuckolded, he is unlikely to forgive her."

Jane nodded. "How sensible you are, Lucy."

With other people's problems, perhaps. But what about her own?

"Come and have tea." Lucy rubbed Jane's back as they walked along the landing. "It is not unheard of for couples to face problems, but they stay married. Look at Lady Caroline Lamb and her husband, for instance."

Jane groaned. "Lady Caroline is completely shameful. I hope it's not her influence that causes Anabel to behave in this manner." She looked thoughtful. "But divorce is not something Howe would welcome. It would tarnish his reputation and might affect his career."

"Then we must wait and hope the matter is resolved one way or the other."

"And before my mother hears of it," Jane said miserably.

Lucy nodded. Aunt Mary was so proud of her girls, she would be greatly distressed to hear about this. And she feared that if

Anabel's foolishness continued, the news of it would reach Aunt Mary's ears.

THE DRIVE HOME in the phaeton had passed without Hugh taking much notice of the scene, his mind still occupied with Lucy. Whether it was her upbringing or inherently who she was, Lucy had the kind of fundamental honesty that made her take responsibility for her own actions. And he supposed that included him. She seemed determined he should not become involved in her problems. He'd wanted to say it was nonsense, and much more, to wrap his arms around her and ease her worries, but he was committed to keeping his silence by his promise to Isabel's father. Isabel's wedding might not go ahead. Would her father finally step in and stop it? To keep his daughter in England? Best Hugh left the city for a spell. When he'd told Lucy, it had been a desperate, last-minute decision to put some distance between him until he could call on her as a free man. He could return before any firm commitment was made by another suitor. If it came to that, he'd have weeks while the banns were read to change her mind. And he had been confident for some time that Lucy felt as he did. He only hoped she wouldn't be pressured by her aunt, although… He smiled. He couldn't see Lucy bowing to pressure.

His accountant had advised him of an investment of his father's. A steelworks in Newcastle, which wasn't doing as well as it should have been, so Hugh needed to look at the company's books and discuss the matter with the manager.

His last evening spent in London. He was restless, and therefore grateful for Luke's invitation to dinner at White's. As they sat drinking wine over a leisurely meal, Hugh noticed his friend seemed as distracted as he was himself.

"I have no title, Hugh," Luke said, over his third glass of claret. His blunt statement came like a bolt of lightning from a clear blue sky. Hugh gazed at him in surprise, struggling to understand the reason for it. Luke looked a little desperate.

"I am aware of that, my friend. What of it?"

"You will want a titled gentleman for Lady Sarah, one with far more than I have to offer."

"Ah. Now I understand." Hugh grinned. "A man who will take good care of my sister means more to me than a title." He thought briefly of Cardew. "If this means you wish to court my sister, you have my full support."

Luke leaned back in his chair, his shoulder sagging with obvious relief. "I find myself in a quandary where Lady Sarah is concerned. She interrupts my sleep."

Hugh nodded. He understood only too well what that meant. "I couldn't be more pleased, Luke. I had wished to see you two together."

Luke leaned forward, his blue eyes intense. "Trouble is, I have no idea if I have a chance with her. Viscount Cardew is probably still in London and won't give her up easily. And I don't trust the fellow. It was all I could do not to plant him a facer in Hyde Park."

"I wouldn't have objected had you done so. But Cardew is to marry Lady Gwendolyn Piper. I suspect his mother is behind the marriage. Hard to see him going against her wishes." His body tensed with the anger and frustration he'd suffered for Sarah's sake. "His mother has always had an iron control over him."

Luke smiled. "Then perhaps I have a chance."

"More than a good one, old fellow." Hugh had noticed Sarah's interest in Luke. But was it too soon for her to put Cardew behind her? "Shall we have another bottle? Or will we go to the card room?"

"Cards. Another bottle and I'll be legless. I'm never good at drinking to excess, so I don't usually imbibe very much."

"I can't afford to get bosky myself. Not when I'm leaving for Newcastle first thing in the morning." Hugh pushed back his chair. He couldn't have been more pleased. Could he leave

London without worrying about Sarah? That was one problem off his mind. But it left him with two others to stew over. His mother's health and Lucy facing the 'cut direct' should her lie be bandied about. Was he being overly protective? It seemed he always had been where she was concerned, and ladies didn't always appreciate that level of interference. "Go and see Sarah soon, Luke."

"Is tomorrow too soon?"

"Perfect."

At the door of the card room, Hugh spied Mr. Rattray seated at a table. "Do you know anything about that fellow in a gray tailcoat and striped waistcoat?"

"Only that he's known not to pay his bills."

"There would be a few here who fail in that regard," Hugh said. Still, it gave him pause to think. The man was unreliable. He remembered their first meeting, watching Rattray charming people. Hugh had taken an immediate dislike to him.

The next morning, he glanced at the few dark clouds on the horizon as his coach left London behind and headed north on the Great Northern Road. He cursed. He didn't relish traveling in bad weather. Even though improvements had been made to the road, mud-filled potholes still caused damage to vehicles and held up traffic. He sat back against the squab, already impatient and wishing he could ride Chance instead of traveling by coach.

What Luke had confessed to him over dinner pleased him a great deal. Now that Sarah had a new suitor, and one he admired, Hugh felt more confident about her resisting any further advances from Cardew, should he make any. Though it would be foolish to think Cardew would give up easily after the scene Luke had described to Hugh at the park. What did he hope to gain from this behavior? Surely, he wouldn't want Sarah for his mistress?

Hugh might even extend the trip a week or two. Travel over the Scottish border to dig into Rattray's past. It was unusual for him to take an instant dislike to anyone, but something about the fellow bothered him, and he didn't like him being anywhere near Lucy. For that matter, he didn't want any of those other fellows who took an interest in Lucy around her, either. But although he had found it extremely difficult not to declare his feelings for her when with her in the phaeton, he'd resisted. It would have come like a bolt out of the blue, and probably shocked her. And he needed time to court her properly. Well, he had now placed himself out of temptation and only hoped that some gentleman didn't snap Lucy up while he was away. It was a risk, but being in London and unable to declare his intentions, he'd be just as hamstrung.

On the afternoon of the third day, after spending a night at a coaching inn where he changed the horses, his coach arrived at Newburn, in Newcastle. The weather was much colder than in London. Wickstaff stepped down and sniffed the air. "It's like comin' home, milord."

"Do you want to return here to live?" Hugh asked his valet.

"When I'm old and gray, perhaps." He looked around. "Shall I head up to that pub on the corner and wait for you?"

"Good idea." Glad of his warm greatcoat, Hugh left Wickstaff and entered the mill to be greeted by a cacophony of noises: men shouting, hammers ringing on metal, whooshing waters, and clouds of steam.

An hour later, he departed after a satisfactory discussion with the manager, Mr. Devlin, who agreed with his views on how to improve productivity and expressed appreciation for his input.

He deliberated on whether to return immediately to London. It was tempting, but Isabel was not yet married, and he wanted to learn more about Rattray for Lucy's sake, so he ordered the coachman to drive on to Scotland.

Chapter Eleven

DURING A LONG week, Lucy heard nothing from Sarah. To appease her aunt on Monday and again on Friday, Lucy rode to the park in Mr. Nash's high-perch phaeton with Maisie, hanging on to the side of the ridiculously high vehicle. Nash called again on Saturday after they'd danced at a ball on Friday evening, and took tea with them.

Lucy considered him very young, and so very conscious of his image among members of the *ton*. She feared he might believe the rumor, now gaining even more credence in London. A guest at the latest ball had asked her about it and another person had spoken of it to her a few evenings ago. She was sick of having to refute it and watch them decide if she was being humble. A lady said she found Lucy's discretion admirable.

But Mr. Nash explained he liked to be seen with her. *"A lot of fellows will envy me, escorting a pretty lady,"* he'd said. It was odd how empty his compliment seemed. As if she might be a new, fancy vehicle or a horse he bought.

It all made her tired, of herself, and of London. She moped until Aunt Mary told her to brighten up and said men disliked sad women. If only she could see Sarah. Perhaps she had news of her brother, but that thought worried her afresh.

On the following Monday, Mr. Rattray came to dinner. Aunt Mary fussed about him, ensuring he had every comfort, as he talked of his close friendship with Viscount Castlereagh. "He often seeks my opinion," he said, which Lucy thought pompous.

"That's no surprise," Aunt Mary said warmly. "His lordship has suffered some criticism, and you have such an excellent grasp of the political issues he must deal with, Mr. Rattray."

Over dessert, and with her aunt out of the room, Lucy, growing tired of his sly glances, questioned him about his family.

He raised his eyebrows. "My, I am surprised to hear you speak at last, Miss Kershaw."

"Do you still have family in Scotland, sir?"

"I do. My brother, Baron Maitland, still lives in the family castle."

Lucy widened her eyes, adopting an enthusiasm she didn't feel. "You grew up in a castle?"

He puffed himself up. "Indeed, I did."

"Can you tell me about it? I've always wanted to visit one."

He glanced at her suspiciously. "You might find them picturesque, but they are, as you would expect, ancient, built of stone with damp, cold drafty corridors and a strong smell of the sea."

"The castle overlooks the sea? How thrilling. I can imagine the waves crashing on the rocks below and the gulls wheeling in the sky. Where is it? On the east coast?"

His eyes refused to meet hers. He cleared his throat and took his time over his wine. "The castle is near Linlithgow, north of Edinburgh. You have probably never heard of it."

It gratified her that her questions had unsettled him. "No, I must confess I haven't," Lucy said, adopting a disappointed manner. "When did you leave and come to London?"

His hard gaze searched hers. "Some years ago. There's no future for a second son there."

He was telling a tall tale, she was sure of it. He spoke as if he'd rehearsed it. "Do you miss it?"

"Not at all. I have a delightful estate in Essex. So much more comfortable." He leaned forward. "I'm sure you and your aunt would enjoy a visit."

"I am certain my aunt would."

"We must discuss it at a later time," he said thoughtfully, tapping the table with his fingertips.

Aunt Mary returned and glanced from Mr. Rattray to Lucy. "Would you ask the maid to remove the dessert plates, please, Lucy? We will take our coffee in the parlor."

Lucy left her aunt merrily chatting. After she gave Maisie the order, she retired to her bedchamber. Mr. Rattray had not liked her questions. She wasn't surprised. He had his secrets. If only she could find a way to uncover them.

She did not go down again. After the front door shut, Aunt Mary came into her bedchamber, frowning. "Were you rude to Mr. Rattray, Lucy? Something seemed to nag at him, and he finally excused himself and left early."

She looked so disappointed, it made Lucy a little guilty. "I merely asked him to tell me more about Scotland."

Aunt Mary nodded thoughtfully. "Very well. When you saw Mr. Nash last, did he say he would call tomorrow?"

"He didn't mention it." Lucy felt only relief. So many hours spent in his company last week had been enough. She doubted he'd fallen madly in love with her. He was more interested in himself and how he appeared to others than with her.

Her aunt gazed into the mirror, tweaking a brown curl on her forehead. "He's persistent. I daresay he will propose soon."

Lucy's throat tightened at the thought. "He's certainly given no indication of it."

Aunt Mary turned from the mirror. "But if he should, will you accept him?"

Lucy sighed. "I don't care for him, Aunt Mary."

"What has that to do with it?" her aunt said crossly. "Affection comes *after* marriage. Being the wife of a prosperous man has great advantages, my girl. Especially when you are in desperate straits."

Lucy gazed at her, horrified. Her aunt was quite right. Her reluctance to encourage Mr. Nash or any other suitor had made her an imposition. The lie appeared to be spreading through the *ton*. It appeared she must marry soon or return to Bath.

"Give it some serious thought before he proposes," her aunt said before leaving the room.

Late next morning, a town carriage drew up outside. At first, fearing it was Mr. Nash, Lucy ran to the window in time to see a footman in livery open the door and Sarah step down onto the pavement. Noticing a curtain twitch from the widowed lady in the house over the road, Lucy hurried out to greet Sarah.

"It is lovely to see you." She noticed worry darkening Sarah's blue eyes. Could it be the dowager countess? "Has something happened?"

"Yes. Would you care to stroll with me in the park? We might speak there where we won't be overheard."

"Of course. Come into the parlor while I get my bonnet and gloves, and tell my aunt."

As they strolled along the paths in Hyde Park, a brisk wind teased at the gray clouds overhead, and the air felt humid, promising rain. Fearing they would have little time for a chat, Lucy turned to her concerned friend. "What is it? Can you tell me?"

"Mr. Beaufort has called several times and took me in his carriage to see the new monument in Green Park. Have you seen it?"

Lucy shook her head.

"The Temple of Concord. It's a folly to mark the signing of the Treaty of Paris and quite extraordinary. There's a brightly painted bridge and pagoda spanning the canal at St. James's Park. Mr. Beaufort was very attentive."

"But that is splendid news, is it not?" Lucy said, confused by Sarah's demeanor.

"I received a letter from Lord Cardew yesterday. He returns to London tomorrow and writes that he is not going to marry Lady Gwendolyn."

"Goodness," Lucy said, gripped by the news. This was entirely unexpected. Admittedly, Sarah was an earl's daughter, but to give up the marriage already arranged to a duke's daughter, a woman of even higher rank? It would cause a dreadful commotion. She doubted Lord Cardew had the fortitude to weather it.

"He says we must elope before his mother finds out."

Lucy stared at her. "He would go against his mother's wishes?" She was immediately suspicious. "Are you sure he is being truthful?"

Sarah shrugged. "He must love me. Otherwise, why would he break off his betrothal to Lady Gwendolyn?"

"I'm sure he does love you, in his way. But might he merely want to get you to himself? Suppose he doesn't mean to marry you?"

Sarah's blue eyes grew dark with distress. She shook her head. "Surely, he wouldn't do such a terrible thing."

"I don't know Lord Cardew, so I can't say what he is capable of. But what about Mr. Beaufort? I'm sure his intentions would be honorable."

"Yes, and I've come to like him a good deal. But Robert says I owe him allegiance. We have been together for so long…"

Lucy took her arm. "You owe him nothing, Sarah. Think what your mother and brother would say and how disappointed they would be should you elope? It will create a dreadful scandal."

"They would accept it in time, and it will be a good marriage. Robert is a viscount and heir to the Skelton earldom."

"I find it difficult to believe him. If he wants to marry you, he should do so in the proper manner, by first speaking to your brother. Not whisk you away from your family and deny you a wedding surrounded by those who love you," Lucy said, deeply concerned for her friend. "Please give it some thought and don't make a hasty decision."

Sarah smiled weakly. "You're right, of course. I will demand more assurances from Robert when he calls to see me tomorrow." Doubt filled her eyes. "Mama has taken to her bed again. She says she is merely tired. The doctor has prescribed a tonic. I wish Hugh would come home."

Lucy's chest fluttered. "Are you expecting him soon?"

"He wrote to say he was venturing farther north but didn't say why. I imagine it's a business matter."

Rain began to patter onto the leaves above them. Sarah put up her umbrella, and they huddled together as they ran for the carriage.

Inside, Sarah put a hand on Lucy's arm. "You are a true friend. There is something else I would like to ask of you."

Lucy smiled. "Certainly."

"Could you come to the house tomorrow and be there when Lord Cardew arrives? I know what I have to say to him, but he tends to browbeat me. He makes me feel that I am at fault, which is ridiculous, I know, but…"

"Of course I will. But I doubt Lord Cardew will be too thrilled by my presence."

Sarah sank back against the squab. "Oh, thank you. I feel better already. I'll send the carriage for you at ten o'clock."

"I'll be ready."

Lucy disembarked, fearing repercussions from Aunt Mary, who waited at the door.

"Mr. Nash called as I expected, Lucy. I don't know why you didn't wait to see him."

"We made no arrangement, Aunt."

"The friendship is advantageous, I grant you, but surely, you don't hope to wed above your station."

Lucy was annoyed. She didn't befriend people for her own aggrandizement. "Lady Sarah has asked me to call tomorrow. She wishes me to help her with a problem," she said in a challenging tone.

"You would be better served spending time with Mr. Nash. He is the only gentleman who seems keen to marry you."

It appeared her aunt was keen to see her married and thought Lucy should focus on finding a husband. But at least she didn't attempt to prevent her from going. Her aunt turned on the stairs.

"It would be impolite to refuse the invitation. But you must be careful not to let Mr. Nash slip through your fingers. You may be sorry when the Season ends, and you go home with nothing to show for it."

HUGH'S COACH BEGAN the long journey from Linlithgow to London. Forced to be patient, his anger gave way to anxiety as he thought of Rattray's lies. The man was an unmitigated scoundrel. Baron Maitland had invited Hugh to dine. In the baronial dining hall with a fire blazing in the huge fireplace, Hugh had put his question to him.

The big, fair-haired man stroked his beard. "Douglas Rattray? Haven't seen him for years. His father worked for me, and Douglas grew up here. But he ran away as soon as he was old enough. I doubt his father heard from him again. The father's gone now, so we can't ask him. Why are you interested in the man?"

"He resides at present in London. Puts it about that he's your brother. And behaves as if he's wealthy."

"Och!" Frowning, he poured them both a glass of Scotch whisky. "I dinnae think Rattray has much money. Though he certainly had a grand opinion of himself even when he was young."

Lightning lit up the sky beyond the tall window, and soon after, heavy rain battered the glass. "You'd best put up here tonight. Wouldn't want you to negotiate the cliff road in the dark with a storm raging. The weather changes quickly here, and it should prove all clear in the morning." Maitland smiled. "And it would be pleasant to have your company for a game of chess."

The next day, the storm had rolled away out to sea, as the baron had predicted. The sun struggled through a bank of clouds as Hugh's coach swayed around the sharp bends in the narrow road. The rocky cliff below was battered by waves. He looked forward to returning to London. Seeing his mother and Sarah and hearing Isabel's news. Would the wedding go ahead as planned? Or had Sir Phillip thought better of it? Might Lady Ashton change her husband's mind by suggesting another solution? Like giving up her baby? She had been determined to keep her daughter in England. Hugh especially wanted to deal with Rattray. He only hoped the gentleman hadn't put whatever plan he had in his mind into action. And he had some scheme in mind, Hugh was sure of it.

He held the strap as the coach lurched around a corner. When would he see Lucy again? She was constantly in his thoughts, her soft, brown eyes, her luscious mouth, and her stern insistence that he wasn't to involve himself in her troubles. She made no secret of it. In the society in which he moved, such spontaneous honesty was rare. People guarded their words, and most were scrupulously polite. And some were not above lying to gain society's favor. Perhaps Lucy had been brought up differently, but it was certainly refreshing. And it was clear when they were close on the dance floor or in his carriage together. She was as drawn to him as he was to her. The air fairly crackled between them. But she was determined to keep him at arm's length. Well, he had interfered in her affairs whether she approved of it or not, but he was sure she'd be relieved to hear the news he brought her.

Chapter Twelve

As Lucy donned her pelisse to enter the Fairburns' carriage, her aunt stood in the entry hall with her arms folded. "Don't forget, we must shop this afternoon for material for your new evening gown."

"But, Aunt, I thought you approved of my friendship with Lady Sarah."

"Rattray warned me that Lord Dorchester is a rake. Apparently, Sir Phillip Ashton has been trying to pin him down to announce he and his daughter's betrothal, but Lord Dorchester is resisting, even when it was arranged some time ago."

She knew instinctively that Rattray had lied to her aunt. And this too, would be untrue. Lucy could not believe that of Lord Dorchester. He had never taken liberties with her, even though she sensed he wanted to.

"But you tell me Lord Dorchester is out of town, so I need not worry," her aunt said.

Lucy could argue no further with her aunt just then. "They have sent a maid to accompany me. I can't keep her waiting."

She felt strangely lightheaded as the fine equipage carried her and the Fairburn maid across London. Aunt Mary was right. She should not grow accustomed to such finery, or the company of an elegant, titled family. They came from a different world. For now, Lucy would concentrate on helping her friend, if she could.

Yet at the park, Lord Cardew had proved he would be difficult to deal with. What Sarah thought Lucy could do, and what she could achieve when faced with an angry viscount, were two different things, and made her a little nervous.

A liveried footman admitted Lucy into the soaring entrance hall. Sarah waited for her, where twin staircases climbed to the upper stories. Appearing flustered, she whisked Lucy to the drawing room. "I hope Lord Cardew doesn't stay long. Mama might come down, and to complicate matters further, Mr. Beaufort has left his card," she said breathlessly as they sat together on the cream, satin sofa.

"Lord Cardew won't be overjoyed to find me here," Lucy warned her again.

Worry rumpled Sarah's smooth forehead. "I want to get this over and done with."

"Then you have made up your mind?"

Sarah nodded. "Let's say I have come to my senses at last."

A loud rap at the door echoed through the house. Minutes later, the butler showed Lord Cardew in. When he gazed at Lucy, he scowled. "Miss Kershaw." After a stiff nod, he ignored her, going to kiss Sarah's hand. "Might we have a moment alone, Sarah?"

Sarah shook her head. "You can speak in front of Lucy. She is very discreet."

Aggrieved, he folded his arms. "I'd rather not."

Lucy grew uncomfortable as a grim silence followed.

"Very well," Sarah said at last. "I'll give you a few minutes, Lord Cardew." She gestured to a chair. "But that's all." She turned to Lucy, her cheeks flushed. "Would you mind waiting outside, Lucy?"

This was what Lucy had feared. She didn't trust Lord Cardew but could do nothing other than shut the door behind her and linger in the hall.

As she stood there, the front door opened, and she heard Mr. Beaufort admitted. Spying Lucy, he approached her, his eyebrows lifted in inquiry, as the butler left them.

She felt foolish at being found hovering in the hall and struggled with what she might say to him. But at that moment, Sarah's shriek made them both turn toward the drawing room doors.

"What the devil?" Mr. Beaufort stared at Lucy. "Is that Lady Sarah? Who is with her?"

"Lord Cardew. Sarah has told him their association is at an end. I'm afraid he isn't taking it too well."

"The deuce!" Mr. Beaufort grasped the door latch and opened the door. Lord Cardew was gripping Sarah's shoulders and shaking her. She struggled against him, tears in her eyes.

Mr. Beaufort strode the length of the room and towered over the young lord. "Unhand Lady Sarah, Cardew."

"You, again!" Lord Cardew sneered. "Still can't mind your own business, Beaufort." He released Sarah and came toward Mr. Beaufort, his fists clenched.

At Lord Cardew's wildly aimed fist, Mr. Beaufort feinted to the left before landing the lord a sharp facer. With a surprised yelp, Lord Cardew staggered back, a hand to his bleeding nose. "You'll regret this, Beaufort."

"No, *you* will, Lord Cardew, should your mother hear of it," Sarah said, gasping for breath. "Please leave. I never want to set eyes on you again."

The butler, Grimsby, burst in, followed by two tall, sturdy footmen. "Are you all right, Lady Sarah?" He gazed around and his expression turned to shock when he saw Lord Cardew holding a bloody handkerchief to his nose.

Sarah straightened her shoulders. "Grimsby, Lord Cardew is leaving."

Grimsby eyed Viscount Cardew unsympathetically. "As you wish, Lady Sarah. John, see his lordship out."

As the footman approached, Lord Cardew scowled at Sarah. "You'll regret this," he shouted, then he spun on his heel, pushed past them, and strode into the hall with John close behind him. The butler followed. A few moments later, the front door banged shut.

"It's mere bluster. It wouldn't serve him well to make a fuss," Lucy said, putting her arm around Sarah's trembling shoulders and leading her over to the sofa. Sitting beside her, Sarah wiped the tears from her cheeks. "I'm very grateful to you, Mr. Beaufort."

"There's really no need," Mr. Beaufort said. "I shouldn't think Lord Cardew will trouble you again."

"We are in need of a drink, James," Sarah said to the footman who stood to attention. "Ratafia, Lucy?" she asked. "Mr. Beaufort?"

"Wine, thank you." Mr. Beaufort took a seat across from them his forehead creased with worry as he studied Sarah.

Sarah's smile wobbled, then she smiled and sat up straight. "I hope Mama didn't hear the commotion. I'm so very relieved it's over."

Mr. Beaufort nodded but made no comment. Lucy also refrained from commenting. A little shocked by the violence the young lord had displayed, she considered her dear friend certainly had a fortunate escape. Did Lord Cardew now believe there was no future for him and Sarah? Lucy hoped he would come to accept it. She'd been struck by the difference between the two men. Lord Cardew was like an overgrown, spoiled, and bad-tempered boy, whereas Mr. Beaufort was very much a gentleman, in complete control of his emotions. And she hadn't missed the way he was looking at Sarah now. The yearning expression in his eyes showed how much he cared for her. She hoped Sarah would come to realize how fortunate she would be if they married.

Shortly afterward, Lucy accepted Sarah's offer to send for a carriage to take her home. She wished to arrive before Aunt Mary found a reason to scold her.

Mr. Beaufort also took his leave. Lucy hoped that without Lord Cardew in the picture, they might discover much in common. Perhaps Sarah would fall in love with him. Lucy liked

Mr. Beaufort very much and believed he would be perfect for Sarah, strong, and protective. *As Lord Dorchester would be.* She sighed.

HUGH'S COACH REACHED London after an absence of more than three weeks. He and Wickstaff were pleased to be back on their feet and free of being cloistered in a rocking coach for hours on end. Hugh collected his mail and inquired of the housekeeper, Mrs. Cruikshank, as to the state of his mother's health. She informed him his mother had left her bed and sat in the morning room, where she worked on her tapestry.

He hurried in to greet her and was relieved to find her color so much improved. "How well you look, Mama."

She smiled as he kissed her cheek. "I am feeling more like my old self. Did you have a good trip?"

He sat in an armchair and sifted through his letters. "Well enough. Where is Sarah?"

"She is walking in the park with Mr. Beaufort," his mother said, appearing slightly perplexed. "She has taken the maid Agnes as chaperone. I'm not sure what happened last Tuesday, while I was confined to my bedchamber, but it appears Lord Cardew has returned to Bath, and Sarah seems perfectly happy about it."

Hugh frowned. "I thought he'd left a while ago."

"Apparently, he did. But he returned and came to see her. I've not been told what occurred, but Grimsby informed me Mr. Beaufort was here at the same time."

Hugh wondered if Sarah would tell him the truth or give him an edited version of events. Luke would be a better bet. He'd invite him to dine and have a game of cards or billiards at the club.

"Oh, and Miss Kershaw was also here," his mother added, her needle poised over her tapestry.

At the mention of her name, Hugh's heart gave a throb and his chest tightened. He was anxious to see her and reassure himself that no man had proposed to her. It appeared that Lucy was the calming influence on Sarah, just as he'd hoped. Cardew had left London, so it appeared the matter was at an end. Hugh wanted to see Lucy. He had news for her aunt about Rattray, and a good deal besides. But he discovered a letter from Isabel in the mail. "Excuse me, Mama. I must go up and remove the travel dust."

"Do you have need of me, milord?" Wickstaff asked, emerging from Hugh's dressing room with his hands full of folded cravats, already restoring order after their journey. Hugh's valet had developed the sonorous tones of his butler. Hugh found it amusing, as he had come from the far north.

"I'll bathe. Put out the dark-blue coat and cream pantaloons. I trust you to choose the waistcoat." His former batman made an excellent valet. He had been invaluable during the war. They'd gone through a lot of action together, and he often wondered if Wickstaff missed it.

Wickstaff allowed himself a small smile as he laid out a change of clothes and prepared the bath, while Hugh sat down to read Isabel's letter, wondering what revelations it contained.

She wrote to inform him the wedding was to take place in Canterbury on the following Saturday and their passage was booked for the next day. *I shall write again when we reach our destination, Hugh,* she wrote. *And tell you all about it.* Hugh folded the letter, deciding to see them off at the docks on Sunday. He wished he could be happy for Isabel but couldn't bring himself to believe she had made a good decision. Obviously, Sir Phillip had consented to the marriage. It seemed the best solution, as Isabel loved the father of her baby, and it would spell ruin to the family should it ever get out. But he still pitied Lady Ashton, who would be distraught over losing her beloved daughter.

The other letters were put aside for his secretary. Hugh's plan to see Lucy must wait. After all, he tended to attract attention wherever he went and had made several trips to her aunt's house. He didn't want any gossip to reach the Ashtons before the new Mrs. Benton sailed.

When he came downstairs having bathed and changed, Sarah was in the morning room with Luke, a footman and a maid serving tea. They were laughing together. Her cheeks were pink, and her eyes sparkled. Luke appeared to be a happy man. Hugh looked forward to finding out what had gone on in his absence. There would be three differing versions, Sarah's, Luke's, and Lucy's, if she consented to reveal it. But learning it from Sarah would be no easier than asking Lucy had been. He'd laugh if the matter weren't so serious.

As Sarah was present, Hugh resisted asking Luke what had occurred. The warning in Luke's eyes intrigued him. But he must leave it until they dined at White's club that evening.

When Luke took his leave, and Sarah went upstairs to see their mother, Hugh left the drawing room for the library and sent for Grimsby and the footman who had been on duty that morning.

The butler came in to the library soon afterward with John. "Yes, milord?"

"What took place when Lord Cardew was here? Anything untoward?"

Grimsby cleared his throat. "John can give you a clearer picture, my lord."

John shuffled his feet. "Er. I believe Mr. Beaufort drew Lord Cardew's cork, milord."

Hugh's eyebrows rose. "Do you know why?"

"No, but by the sound of it, Lord Cardew caused a lot of trouble," Grimsby said.

"Was this in front of the ladies?"

"Yes, milord."

Hugh nodded. "Thank you, Grimsby, John. That will be all."

It was time to have it out with Sarah. He sat thinking over what he had learned, then when he heard her coming down the stairs, he went out to meet her. "Mama seems better," he said.

"Her health has improved a lot, and the doctor is very pleased."

"Excellent news. Will you come into the library for a moment, Sarah?"

She looked wary. "What for?"

"A drink, and a chat."

She followed him inside and sat, her feet tucked up at one end of the sofa while Hugh poured the drinks.

He returned to hand her a glass of Ratafia. Carrying his snifter of brandy, he took his favorite chair. "I am told Cardew came here yesterday and caused quite a commotion. Mr. Beaufort had to restrain him. I am sorry I wasn't here. Did he threaten you, Sarah? Should I teach him a lesson?"

"He will have scurried back to Bath by now." A reluctant smile curled Sarah's lips. "You should have seen it, Hugh. Lord Cardew tried to punch Mr. Beaufort, but he didn't have a chance because Mr. Beaufort was so quick on his feet. Lord Cardew's bloodied nose subdued him admirably."

"What was Cardew's reason for making such a fool of himself?"

"He came to tell me he is not marrying Lady Gwendolyn Piper." She looked evasive staring down at her glass, but he didn't press her. "But his mother hadn't been told of this decision. I didn't believe him, so I asked him to leave."

"That was wise of you, Sarah."

"Yes. I was glad to have Lucy here. She is able to see things more clearly than I do. I become too emotional."

"It's hard for anyone to end a long-standing relationship, Sassie."

"Yes." She rubbed her eyes. "But I am sure I did the right thing."

"I'm sure of it too." He held up his glass. "Let's drink to the future."

She smiled and raised her glass, then took a sip. "I wonder

what the future holds for you, Hugh?"

"It's a little unclear at the moment."

She fought a smile. "Lucy tells me Mr. Nash is becoming serious. Her aunt believes he will propose."

Hugh cursed under his breath. "He's not the man for her."

She raised her eyebrows. "Who would be the right one, I wonder?"

He ignored her provocative remark. "I've seen Nash at the gambling tables. He's reckless. He'll go through his inheritance in no time." Hugh rose. As he passed her, he reached down to tap her nose. "You'll be one of the first to hear my future plans, when I know them myself."

Chapter Thirteen

"WILL YOU MARRY me, Miss Kershaw?"

Lucy's throat tightened. Mr. Nash had actually proposed. They were walking in the park with the maid, Maisie, looking bored, trailing behind them, when he'd led her to a wooden bench. After a quick glance at the dusty path, he sat beside her, apparently deciding not to risk the knee of his yellow pantaloons. She was glad of that, for he would only feel more foolish when she refused him.

He had voiced the opinion that as husband and wife, they would make a striking couple, so Lucy had expected this and was prepared. While aware it left her in a difficult position once her aunt heard of it, she gently refused him.

He looked shocked. "Have I been too hasty?"

"Not at all, sir. It's just that I don't believe we'd suit," Lucy said, relieved that he didn't attempt to seize her and try to kiss her, or declare he would die without her. In fact, he had not mentioned love at all. "We are so very different," she said gently.

He ran a hand through his fair hair, evidently perplexed, then, squinting in the sunlight, replaced his hat. "We are? In what manner?"

"I enjoy reading. By your strong arms and broad shoulders, it is obvious that you are an athletic gentleman who prefers to be outdoors."

He nodded, seemingly slightly mollified by her flattery. "Yes, I prefer riding and fencing to reading. To be truthful, I had enough of books at Eton. But I fail to see it as a problem."

"I fear I should bore you," Lucy confessed, when in essence it was she who would find marriage to him tedious.

Subdued, when he'd taken her home, he made no further argument.

Lucy arrived grimly, prepared to face her aunt, and entered the house. Puzzled and alarmed by the sound of loud sobbing, she hurried into the drawing room. Aunt Mary lay prostrate on the sofa, with Mr. Rattray leaning over her, patting her arm and uttering soothing words.

Jane, who hovered nearby, turned to Lucy with tears in her eyes. "Viscount Howe sent word that Anabel has run away with her lover, a Mr. Connor."

"And who is he? Certainly, no one of importance! We are ruined!" Aunt Mary shrieked. "I can never show my face in London again!"

Deeply upset for her aunt, Lucy hurried over to her. "How distressing, Aunt Mary. When Anabel sees the error of her ways, I'm sure she will return. I hope few learn of it. How long have they been gone?"

"Several weeks," Jane said. "According to Lord Howe, she left a note. She traveled to Ireland with Mr. Connor."

Lucy glanced sympathetically at her aunt. It appeared impossible to avoid a scandal.

"That heathenish country," Aunt Mary wailed. "Why on Earth would they go there?"

"Mr. Aidan Connor is Irish," Jane explained. "Lord Howe has made it clear he will not take her back."

"I'll never see my little girl again." Aunt Mary sobbed, her voice muffled by the handkerchief. "What if something happens to her? How will I know?"

"Once she's settled, she is sure to write." Lucy recalled how unhappy Anabel had appeared. Didn't Jane say that Howe had taken a mistress? Yet he would suffer no condemnation from his peers. How unfair life was to women.

"Miss Kershaw is right," Mr. Rattray said soothingly, nodding his approval at Lucy. "Your daughter is sure to miss her mama."

This seemed to make things worse for Aunt Mary, who burst into a fresh fit of sobbing. "And I won't be with her!"

"Mama, please come upstairs and lie down," Jane said. "I'll tell Maisie to bring you some tea and put a warming pan in your bed."

Unsteady, Aunt Mary stood, assisted by Mr. Rattray's arm. "Yes, I will lie down. I am quite weak and giddy."

Jane led her mother from the room.

Making no attempt to leave, Mr. Rattray remained with Lucy.

She moved quickly to the door. "Goodbye, Mr. Rattray, thank you for your kind attentions to my aunt. We are grateful for your discretion. I must go up and see if there's anything I can do."

He moved to open it for her, then stood too close as she passed through into the hall. "I think it would be wise for your aunt to leave London and spend a pleasant few days in the country. I shall mention it to her when she is calmer."

As Mrs. Boyce, the housekeeper, was with her aunt, and young William, their man-of-all-work, nowhere to be seen, Lucy saw Mr. Rattray to the front door, just as Mr. Nash's phaeton pulled up.

"I see you have a visitor," Mr. Rattray said dourly. "Shall I send him away?"

She stiffened at his impudence. "No, thank you. I shall see the gentleman."

Mr. Rattray donned his hat and walked away, as Mr. Nash, carrying a glove, joined her at the door. He glanced at Mr. Rattray's retreating figure. "You dropped this, Miss Kershaw."

"Oh, so I did. Thank you for returning it." She had been in such haste to leave him that hadn't noticed.

He hovered. "I wondered if you might have thought things

over and had a change of heart?" He eyed the door behind her. "It was a little rushed. We might talk about it."

"I see no point, Mr. Nash. My mind is made up. I cannot invite you to have tea. My aunt received distressing news. I should go up to her in case she needs me."

He lifted his shoulders with a heavy sigh. "So that's that, then."

Lucy's stomach churned. "I am sorry," she repeated. "I really must go to her," she said, a hand on the door latch.

"Very well. I'll return in a few days and see how things are." He donned his hat and bade her a reluctant goodbye.

Lucy forced a smile and waited until he'd taken up the reins and driven off. Then she slipped back inside and shut the door with palpable relief. She hoped he'd think twice about calling again.

Climbing the stairs, she wondered if Mr. Rattray meant to marry her aunt and carry her away to the country? If that were the case, Lucy would have to return to Bath. The thought of leaving brought Lord Dorchester to mind again. Had he returned safely from his trip? She hoped to hear from Sarah soon.

The next day, Aunt Mary remained in bed. She moaned in distress. It upset Lucy to see her aunt so troubled, but there was little she could do other than try to make her comfortable.

Lucy was halfway up the stairs to see if her aunt needed anything when horses' hooves and the jingle of a carriage sounded on the road outside. She groaned. Was it Mr. Nash calling again? When the knocker sounded, she paused, a hand on the banister, trying to think of a way to deter him. William appeared from the direction of the kitchen, busily chewing, and went to open the front door and admitted Lord Dorchester.

So relieved to see him, Lucy hurried down, suffering the overwhelming desire to throw herself into his arms. The way he looked at her made her catch her breath, sure he could read the effect he had on her in her eyes. "It is good to see you, Lord Dorchester." She stepped down onto the hall floor. "Did you have a good journey, my lord?"

He handed his hat and gloves to William, then turned to observe her once more, searching her face. For what? Signs of poor sleep? She hadn't slept well because of Mr. Rattray's announcement, and there was Mr. Nash, who didn't seem prepared to accept her refusal, to contend with. She was sure he didn't love her. Was her rejection a blow to his vanity?

"Thank you. It was successful." He smiled at her approvingly. "No need to ask how you are, Miss Kershaw. You look in the pink of condition."

So she was horribly flushed, she thought, annoyed. "I am a little flustered," she admitted. "We are at sixes and sevens here." As William had left them, she led Lord Dorchester into the drawing room. "Do please be seated. Would you care for a libation?"

"No, thank you." He sat on a chintz-covered armchair and leaned forward, his hands on his muscular thighs, drawing her eye there and making her aware of their pleasing shape. "I'm sorry to hear that. What has occurred?" he said.

They were alone. Where was her aunt? Seated opposite him, she wondered if Aunt Mary would approve if she told him, or think Lucy dreadfully remiss. But Lord Dorchester would be discreet. He had already shown he was well able to keep a secret. "My cousin, Lady Anabel Howe, has left her marriage and run away with a gentleman. My aunt is very upset."

He frowned. "I'm sure she would be, poor lady. Can you tell me more?"

"Anabel has fled to Ireland with Mr. Aidan Connor, who is unknown to us. My aunt is heartbroken. She believes she will neither hear from her daughter again, nor know how she fares. Aunt Mary is concerned that Lord Howe might seek a divorce."

He leaned forward, concern in his blue eyes. "Would you like me to look into the matter? I might discover their precise destination. Would that bring your aunt some comfort?"

She feared she was coming to depend on him. And that could

only end badly. "I believe it would, especially if she learns Anabel is happy and well. But really, is that even possible? They have been gone for weeks."

He stood. "Let me see what I can do."

Lucy rose too. "You are so very good, Lord Dorchester."

His smile was enigmatic. "Am I?"

She laughed. "You must know it. I am constantly indebted to you. How can I ever repay you?"

He held out a hand to her and smiled. "I wouldn't feel too downhearted. Something might come up."

What did that mean? Did he see her in his future in some way? Deciding to worry about that later, she placed her hand in his elegant, long-fingered one, twice the size of hers, the palm edged with a roughness, which she liked. It showed he didn't live an idle, pampered life like so many gentlemen she'd met. For a moment, they stood while she fought to concentrate, disturbed by their closeness and his suggestion of a future relationship, whatever that may entail. Her heart thudded so fast in her chest, she feared she would collapse into his arms. Their eyes met, his so blue, they made her breathless. "I am most grateful, my lord, and I know my aunt will be."

"It's no trouble for me to make a few inquiries." He released her hand, and with a slight bow, walked to the door.

Lucy thought otherwise. She was sure he was a busy man, but she didn't like to argue with him. She could only be grateful.

He picked up his hat and gloves from the hall table, and she opened the front door. Because William had disappeared into the kitchen once again where delicious aromas wafted out. The cook must have been baking.

Once he had driven away, Lucy hurried up the stairs to give Aunt Mary the news. Just knowing Lord Dorchester might be able to help would give her aunt some hope.

A hand on the bedchamber door latch, Lucy suddenly wondered why she'd never asked him why he'd called. Whatever the reason, it must wait until she saw him again. It thrilled her to think that she would. There seemed no end to her foolishness.

IT HAD BEEN the wrong time to broach the subject of Mr. Rattray, Hugh quickly realized. Lucy had looked so worried about her aunt. It was all he could do not to draw her into his arms and comfort her. If he could provide some information which might ease her aunt's anxiety, he would certainly do so. He intended to ask an Irish friend if he might have heard of this Mr. Connor. There were a few other avenues to pursue.

He suspected Sarah's explanation of Cardew's visit was not the full story. He'd wanted to ask Lucy about it but had refrained because not only had it been the wrong time, but she probably wouldn't have told him much. His best bet was Luke, and he would find out more tonight. If necessary, he would ferret out Lord Cardew, if he had not yet left London, and teach him a lesson he wouldn't forget in a hurry.

That evening at the club, Luke was quite forthcoming. "The man is a bully," he said as they drank claret in the library. "He faced up to me, so I was forced to subdue him. Drew his cork."

"Splendid." Hugh grinned. "He's been intolerably spoiled by his mother. Thinks he can have anything he wants. Well, he can't have Sarah."

Luke frowned. "I trust she isn't too upset? Doesn't hold it against me?"

"I don't believe so. She says you and Miss Kershaw were very supportive."

"Miss Kershaw was. In my opinion, a lady to have in your corner."

"Quite." Hugh wanted that, and much more. In a few days, he would know if Lucy felt the same. She wasn't the flirtatious type who would toy with a man's emotions. Probably she'd set him straight on a matter when she thought he was mistaken. But dash it all, he found even that attractive, as well as the many other fine qualities he'd discovered about her. The sooner she married him, the better he'd like it. He felt like a schoolboy lusting after the unattainable. As he had not heard from Isabel or her parents again, it appeared that after this Saturday, he would be free.

Chapter Fourteen

THE HOUSEKEEPER, MRS. Boyce came into the breakfast room where Lucy was eating toast. "Your aunt wishes to see you. She's in her bedchamber, miss."

Lucy abandoned her breakfast and went upstairs. She was surprised to find Aunt Mary and Maisie in a flurry of activity, sorting through her gowns, bonnets, and Spencers. It was the first time since Anabel had run away with her lover that her aunt had smiled. "There you are, Lucy. I have the most pleasant news. Mr. Rattray has sent a note this morning. He has to visit his country house and has invited us to accompany him. Are we not fortunate?" She examined the hem of the plum velvet evening gown she held for tears. "I cannot leave you in London unchaperoned. Maisie will help you pack enough clothes for three days. An evening gown too, of course. I am sure we will dress for dinner. The carriage is to call for us at five o'clock."

Lucy's heart sank. "I'll go and do it now, Aunt Mary."

"Good. Take your night things in a separate bag, as Mr. Rattray plans to spend a night at an inn on the way."

Surely, this meant Mr. Rattray was about to ask her aunt to marry him. While Lucy was pleased to see her aunt happy, she wished it was another gentleman and not one whom she simply could not like. Lucy suspected lies tripped smoothly from Mr. Rattray's lips, seemingly of long practice. She was unsure of his motive but doubted it was passion for her aunt. If only she could have made her aunt aware of it, but the chance to trip him up in a lie seemed to have gone. And her aunt was so vulnerable now after Anabel's elopement that she grasped at the chance for happiness.

Nearing five o'clock, William, groaning in a manner Lucy thought unnecessary as her portmanteau wasn't very heavy, carried it down the stairs to add to her aunt's luggage at the front door.

Precisely on the hour, a carriage pulled up outside. "Here is Mr. Rattray." Aunt Mary hurried down, fiddling with the lace collar on her best traveling gown. "Smile, Lucy, and make yourself agreeable to the gentleman."

William opened the door to Mr. Rattray. He entered the hall, rubbing his hands, his servant following. There was a gleam in Mr. Rattray's usually opaque gray eyes. He kissed her aunt's hand then hovered over Lucy's, the smell of pomade from his red hair pervading the air. "It will be quite cool this evening. I hope you are rugged up well, ladies. We have quite a distance to travel before we can put up for the night."

"We are looking forward to this delightful excursion, Mr. Rattray," Aunt Mary said, fluttering her eyelashes girlishly. "It is so kind of you to invite us."

"Not at all, Mrs. Grayswood." He went over to Lucy, who was donning her pelisse. "May I be of assistance, Miss Kershaw?"

"No, thank you, sir." She pulled it on hastily, not wanting his hands on her.

"Good, then we'll be off, shall we?" He motioned sharply to "his man," as he referred to his servant, to pick up their luggage. He was a rough-looking fellow with shabby clothes and greasy hair. Lucy felt uneasy, but her aunt was so keen to leave, there was nothing she could say.

Outside, his carriage waited. The coachman sat hunched on the box, his hat pulled low over his face. Lucy thought the vehicle quite shabby for that of a well-to-do gentleman. But perhaps it had become splashed with mud on the journey here. When she was helped inside, the stale smell from the squabs made her catch her breath.

Aunt Mary was gayly laughing at something Mr. Rattray said and didn't seem to notice. She settled a bandbox with her best bonnet into a corner and sat next to Lucy, smoothing her gloves. Mr. Rattray followed them inside and took the seat opposite with his back to the horses. He thumped the roof with his cane, and the coachman's whip cracked as he cried, "Walk on."

Lucy looked upon this trip as something to be endured. But she would try not to spoil it for her aunt, who looked forward to it so eagerly.

As the carriage set off down the road, it was still light. The sun would not set until close to eight o'clock. "Where are we to spend the night?" Lucy asked, wondering how long she had to breathe in the stale air tinged with Mr. Rattray's pomade. She had opened a window but closed it again when her aunt had put a hand to her bonnet and complained it was too breezy.

"A quaint inn, just outside St. Albans. You'll find it both comfortable and charming, Miss Kershaw," he said in jocular tones. "As we travel farther, we will pass through Cambridge, a wonderful historic town I'm sure you'll enjoy exploring."

"Indeed we will," Aunt Mary said firmly, raising her eyebrows at Lucy.

"It sounds delightful." Lucy tried to sound convincing, although it was hardly the truth, while Mr. Rattray fussed over her aunt, covering her knees with a rug.

An hour later, Aunt Mary's head began to nod. Lucy was sure her aunt had not slept well since the dreadful news about Anabel had reached them. In the stuffy air and with the rocking motion, she grew a little sleepy too, but for some reason she couldn't quite define, she needed to be alert. Fortunately, Mr. Rattray folded his arms and sank into a silent stupor, not appearing to require any conversation from her. The miles passed by.

Nearing eight o'clock, the sun sank behind the horizon and

night fell. Beyond the window, the sky was a vast, black arch overhead where a crescent-shaped moon hung suspended. The coach lanterns had been lit, sending a feeble glow over the dark road.

Lucy wondered again why Lord Dorchester had come to see her the other day, and if he had discovered anything about Anabel's whereabouts that would give her poor aunt some relief.

Sometime later, the carriage pulled into the forecourt of an ancient brick inn, surrounded by woodland. The building appeared alarmingly ramshackle, at least from the outside. Her aunt woke with a loud snort. "Are we here already? My, that took no time at all."

Mr. Rattray helped her aunt down, then Lucy followed quickly unaided. They were escorted into the inn and greeted by the innkeeper, as if they had entered the Prince Regent's Carlton House. The inn proved as dismal inside as it did out, the furniture in need of a dust and cobwebs dangling in the draft. If her aunt was disappointed, she gave no indication of it. They were shown into a small parlor and served a late supper of bread and butter and cauliflower soup. Mr. Rattray flourished a bottle of wine he had brought with him for the occasion, which he declared was an excellent vintage. He poured her aunt a glass, but despite him seeming offended by her refusal, Lucy still declined it.

"I expect you have yet to develop a taste for good wine," Mr. Rattray said, his mouth pulled down.

After they ate the small meal served by a surly, silent servant, she and her aunt were shown up to their bedchamber, which her aunt insisted she share for propriety's sake. Lucy was glad of the company.

Aunt Mary still appeared exhausted, her movements heavy and slow as they washed, brushed their hair, and changed into nightgowns. They climbed into the lumpy, double bed and her aunt blew out the candle.

In the dark, Aunt Mary tittered. "I hope there are no bed bugs. Even the best inns have them. I usually bring my own sheets, but it was such a rush."

Lucy feared it too, but as soon as they'd settled down, her aunt began to snore, and Lucy resigned herself to a sleepless night. But after only a short time, Lucy's eyelids grew heavy, and she drifted into sleep.

Waking suddenly, she had no idea how long she'd been asleep as she stared into the dark. Had she heard a noise? Lying still, she listened. Aunt Mary was still deeply asleep, and Lucy didn't like to disturb her by lighting a candle. When she'd convinced herself there was nothing to concern her and was settling down again, the door opened and someone entered, holding a lantern. Mr. Rattray's face appeared in the light above it looking ghoulish.

Fear tightened her chest and she gasped. "Is something wrong?" Lucy prodded her aunt, but she didn't stir.

Before she knew it, he was beside her. "I wish you'd drunk the wine. It would make this so much easier," he said, his voice a low growl.

She opened her mouth to scream and was silenced by a sharp blow to her chin. Darkness descended.

⇶⇷

HUGH GAINED SOME helpful news from an Irish friend. Apparently, Aidan Connor, the man with whom Mrs. Grayswood's daughter had run off, had come from Killarney, and it was likely that the couple had gone there. He drove to Westminster and knocked on that lady's front door. The dark-haired young servant, clutching a sugared bun, answered it. "Mrs. Grayswood and Miss Kershaw are away, milord," he said, swallowing noisily. "They left yesterday for the country, for a few days."

That seemed sudden. Lucy had made no mention of it when Hugh had seen her only two days ago. "Where in the country, precisely?"

"Cambridge, I heard it said, milord. Mr. Rattray has a house somewhere in those parts." The boy made a clumsy bow and shut the door.

Rattray! Fear rocketed through him. What was the fraudulent man's intention? It made no sense that someone of his ilk would pursue Lucy's aunt for marriage. She wasn't a wealthy woman. And he didn't believe it was a powerful emotion like love. But curse it, Rattray might believe Lucy was coming into money! Wanting to go in pursuit, Hugh climbed back into the phaeton and took up the reins. But could he in all conscience follow them? Rattray might be entirely innocent of any trickery. But it still left him deeply concerned for Lucy's safety.

If everything went as planned, Isabel would have left England next week. Hugh drove home wondering what he might do and came to the conclusion there was nothing. Lucy was not alone—her aunt was with her. But the rest of the day was spent wishing he'd told her about Rattray. Needing to air his concerns, he decided to seek Luke's opinion.

Luke had told him he would ride today if the fine weather continued. Reaching home, Hugh took up the groom and headed to the park. He drove to the South Carriage Drive and looked for Luke riding in Rotten Row.

Hugh spied him on horseback in a group of friends and hailed him. Handing the reins to the groom, the earl leapt down from the carriage and crossed to the Row, where Luke waited for him, his companions having ridden on.

"I have a problem," Hugh said, when he reached Luke, seated on a tall thoroughbred. Luke dismounted, and they walked into the parkland while he explained.

"I don't see that there's anything I can do," he confessed. "If I'm wrong, Rattray could cause a fuss, just when Sir Phillip Ashton wants Isabel's wedding to go unnoticed."

"If you decide to go, I'll come with you," Luke said thoughtfully. "But how are we to find them? Cambridge isn't small, and his home might be in any of the surrounding villages."

"That's true," Hugh said with a worried nod.

"I'll excuse myself from my party and join you at your home," Luke said. "We'll think more on it, there."

"I appreciate it. Thanks, Luke." Hugh ran back to the phaeton.

As he approached the gates of Dorchester Court, he saw a small figure huddled against the stone wall. He pulled up the horses and Mrs. Grayswood, red-faced, struggling for breath, her bonnet askew, ran over to him.

"It's Mr. Rattray," she gasped out. "Lord Dorchester, forgive me for this intrusion, but I didn't know who else to turn to. *What have I done?*" she wailed.

Hugh leapt down, his heart in his mouth and took her arm leading her through the gates. He would have preferred his mother or Sarah to help, but they were away shopping. "Come inside and have some tea. Then tell me what has happened."

Luke joined them in the drawing room, where Mrs. Grayswood sipped the tea. She had recovered enough to explain. "Mr. Rattray invited me to spend a few days at his country house." She drew in a breath, stark fear in her eyes. "I thought the invitation perfectly respectable with Lucy accompanying us. And I couldn't leave her alone at home."

"Of course," Hugh said in an encouraging tone, although he clamped on his jaw and wanted to shake her to hurry her along.

"We stopped at an inn near St. Albans for the night. At supper, Mr. Rattray produced a bottle of wine he'd brought with him. I drank some, although Lucy declined it." Her eyes widened. "It made me dreadfully drowsy, and as soon as my head hit the pillow, I was asleep." She took another sip of tea, her hand shaking, then put it down carefully. "When I woke in the morning, I had a horrible taste in my mouth and a throbbing headache, and... Lucy was gone!" She stared at them each in turn. "Imagine what a state I was in! I questioned the innkeeper, who said Mr. Rattray had left during the night. He had taken Lucy with him." She dropped her chin to her chest with a sob. "I didn't know what to do. Then I thought of Lady Sarah, who is such a good friend of Lucy's, and called for a carriage to bring me back to London." She glanced at Hugh hopefully.

"I'm afraid my sister isn't here, Mrs. Grayswood."

She clutched her trembling hands. "Then will you help me find her, Lord Dorchester?"

Hugh's chest tightened and he gripped the arm of the chair, his knuckles turning white. He forced himself to sound calm or the lady would be in hysterics. "You can rely on me, Mrs. Grayswood. Do you know where Mr. Rattray's country house might be?"

She mournfully shook her head. "That's the trouble. He must have lied to me. He said it was near Cambridge. But we were nowhere near St. Albans, as he had said. On the way back to London in the carriage I hired, I saw a sign saying Chigwell and Epping Forest, which was only fifteen miles away. Rattray did say his home is surrounded by forest." She sighed. "That's all I am able to tell you. Does it help at all?"

Hugh stood and came to pat her shoulder. Indeed it does." He glanced at Luke. "Fancy taking a drive to Chigwell, Luke?"

"Indeed, I do," Luke said, his tight voice revealing his anger.

"I hope you find her soon, before…" Mrs. Grayswood's voice faltered into silence and her shoulders heaved.

Hugh felt as if he was pulled into a nightmare. He could not lose the woman he adored before he had even had a chance to tell her, to hold her, to make her his own. "I will do my best to find her, Mrs. Grayswood. I'll arrange for my groom to take you home."

"Thank you, my lord. You are very good," she said tearfully, her handkerchief balled in her fist.

He hesitated, wondering if he should mention her daughter's whereabouts, then decided more was needed to be done to find her, and the poor lady had enough to contend with.

Hugh left the room with Luke.

"Surrounded by forest, eh?" Luke said. "So, somewhere near

Epping Forest, then?"

"It's all we have to go on," Hugh said despairingly as he stalked the carpet. "That would mean close to Chigwell, Chingford, or Epping, which narrows it down to several villages." Had he attacked her? That bloody monster, Rattray! He'd throttle the man with his bare hands.

Chapter Fifteen

L UCY GENTLY INVESTIGATED her aching chin. Her head ached as well. Aware of a rocking sensation, she opened her eyes. She was back in the smelly carriage again. The sky beyond the window was gray and tinged with gold and pink as the sun rose. Mr. Rattray sat opposite, watching her. Her stomach lurched, and she feared she might be sick. She lifted the rug over her lap and saw she was wrapped in her dressing gown.

"I haven't touched you, Miss Kershaw," he said, as if he should be applauded. "I won't until we are married. If you mind your manners."

She stared at him. "You think I'll marry you? Are you mad?"

"Not at all. I have planned this to perfection."

"Where is my aunt? Have you hurt her?"

"Merely a little laudanum. It would have given her a good sleep."

She clenched her jaw in anger and then winced. He'd bruised her when he'd hit her. "You are a scoundrel. I always knew it." Lucy looked around for something to hit him with. Her feet were bare. Where were her shoes? She must get away somehow. But there was nothing within reach, not even her luggage. She would have to bide her time.

"We will arrive within an hour or two," he said. "You'd best rest until then."

"Cambridge? So soon?"

He shook his head with a sly smile. "Epping Forest, my dear. I have rented a cottage near there."

"You are a fraud," she said. "You're not wealthy at all. This carriage is the best you can afford. And I'm sure you have no country estate." She sagged back against the squab. This was all her fault. He believed her lie and thought her wealthy. If she insisted she wasn't, would he believe her? Or might he kill her? Chilled to the bone, she tightened her lips, lest she say something wrong. If only she could think, and plan, but she was still woozy.

He leaned forward, with a menacing expression. "You'd best watch yourself. It's not wise to anger me."

Lucy glared at him but fell silent. Best not to fight with him now. She would wait until they arrived. But her hopes faded at the thought of escaping through the forest with no one to turn to for help.

Another hour passed in silence. Finally, the carriage slowed, then turned onto a rutted drive deep within trees and dense shrubbery. They rocked along from pothole to pothole until Lucy became queasy. Then the carriage emerged into a clearing and stopped before a wooden cabin. It looked like a rudimentary hunting hut with shutters over the windows. No smoke came from the one chimney on the moss-covered roof.

Lucy gasped. It was even worse than she'd expected. Who would ever find her here? And who was searching for her? She feared no one. Had her aunt returned to London and gone for help? She wished she was confident of that. But even if they came after Rattray, how would they find them?

The groom opened the door and put down the step. "Out you go," Rattray said, giving her a push.

Lucy glared at the groom, who merely shrugged. The muddy ground had no discernable path to the front door. Lucy's toes squished in the icy puddles, her feet freezing. She shivered as her kidnapper followed her out of the carriage and took her by the elbow, urging her along toward the cabin.

She pulled away from him and turned to speak to the coach-man, who had remained on the box. "This man is abducting me against my will!" she yelled at him. The groom sniggered while the coachman shrugged.

"We want our twenty pounds, Rattray," he snarled. "We got you here by dawn, as promised. Pay up if you want us to take you the rest of the way."

Rattray cursed and pulled bills from his pocket. "Here's half. That's enough for lodgings for the night. You'll get the rest at the end of the journey," he said as the groom came to snatch them up. "Change the horses and don't get drunk at the tavern. We leave tomorrow at first light," he warned. "And we have a good deal farther to go." His hand tightened painfully on Lucy's arm as he dragged her toward the door. She blinked tears away as she stumbled along.

The groom dumped Lucy's belongings inside the door.

The cabin was every bit as bad as she'd feared. Thick dust covered everything, even the wooden walls. The soot-laden air smelled of damp. Shivering, Lucy looked longingly toward the fireplace. A pile of ashes filled the grate, an iron cooking pot hanging above it. She'd tracked mud over the bare boards, which hadn't been swept or washed in years, with her cold, bare feet. There was only a soiled sofa, two threadbare chairs, and a table with a pair of candlesticks and a tinder box. *The one other door must lead to the sleeping quarters*, she thought as a shudder passed down her spine. No light entered through the shuttered windows. Perhaps the other room had a window without shutters. She could climb out during the night.

"The shutter is bolted shut in there too," Rattray said, as if guessing her thoughts. He locked the door and tucked the key in his waistcoat pocket. He gestured to the sofa. "Sit down, and if you give me no trouble, I'll let you dress, and we'll keep the peace until tomorrow."

"You can't marry me. I won't agree to it," Lucy said, sitting gingerly on the sofa. It sagged beneath her.

"Leave that to me."

"Where are we going?"

"Carlisle, then Scotland."

She gaped at him. "Scotland? You *are* mad."

His face went an ugly red, and Lucy shivered. He frightened her. He always had, she realized. If only Aunt Mary had seen that in him, too. Aunt Mary? Had he hurt her? "Where is my aunt?" she demanded.

"On her way back to London, I should think," he said with an indifferent shrug.

"Aunt Mary will contact Bow Street," she warned him. "They will come after you."

"Perhaps, but that will take days. She would have to engage a Bow Street Runner, and just supposing he discovered our trail, which is unlikely, for no one has set eyes on you since we left London except the innkeeper and his servant, we shall be over the border by then."

"Why do you want to marry me?" Lucy asked in desperation. "As you've planned this, you must have looked into the rumor and know I am not an heiress."

"Not yet, you're not," he said over his shoulder while he inspected the wood box.

"What do you mean?"

He removed the two remaining logs and put them in the grate. Then lit the fire. "Your father will be the Marquess of Berwick before the year is out. And I'm a patient fellow."

He straightened and looked at her, that gleam back in his eyes, which she'd come to dread. "That's nonsense. The Marquess of Berwick is a widower," she said. "He has two young sons."

He shook his head. "One son now, for Giles just died. Unfortunately, Berwick and his other son, Sebastian, won't last long. They are gravely ill."

She stared at him, shocked. "I don't believe you!"

"You will, when we get to Carlisle."

"What could have happened to them?"

"I heard it's poisoned water. Killed one of the staff, too. Very sad."

"Poisoned water?" Her stomach roiled. Had he killed a child? "How do you know this? There's been no mention of it in London."

"I have connections in Carlisle."

She put a hand to her stomach, fearing she'd gag, filled with utter terror unlike anything she'd ever experienced before. "Connections? A murderous servant in your pay? You are wicked!"

"I cannot take credit for it," he said, unaffected by her accusation. "I've been in London for months. Any number of people would attest to it. And who would be interested in me? They might focus on your father, however. After all, he will inherit the estate."

Lucy's blood ran cold. "That's absurd," she gasped out, her fingers digging into her palms, wanting to hit him, to wipe the smug look off his face. "My father would never do such a thing, and he couldn't. He lives in Bath."

"But if proof is presented to the magistrate that he hired someone…in the form of a letter, perhaps…" He left the sentence hanging, a sneer curling his lips. "If he agrees to my terms and keeps his word, I shan't send it, of course."

"Forged letters? No one would believe it. Your plan will fail, and you'll end up in Newgate."

He raised his eyebrows, but his eyes had grown dark and angry. "Wait and see," he spat out. "It will all become clear to you."

Lucy, speechless, realized she beheld the devil. But he would not win. He mustn't. Absolute terror racketed through her. She put a hand to her nape and found it wet with sweat. "I want to wash and dress. My feet are muddy, and I'm cold." Her voice faltered, and she feared she would faint, but she gripped the sofa and glared at him. "I presume you have brought my luggage? I want to dress."

Rattray chuckled. "Yes, *milady*." He nodded toward the door. "You can change in there. I'll bring you your luggage and a bowl of water."

"No. First, put the water and my luggage in the room," she said, folding her arms.

Rattray frowned but went outside to the pump. Lucy opened the other door and darted inside, hoping to find a window, but it was as Rattray had said, bolted shut. The shadowy room smelled just as bad as the other, perhaps worse. It didn't bear thinking about as she stared at the narrow cot and its frayed coverlet. A table sat beside it with a stub of candle in a candlestick. Could she get hold of the tinderbox? Would he light it for her? If she could set the cabin on fire, she could escape into the forest. Rattray might be cruel and a ruthless murderer of children, but he wasn't stupid. He had the cunning of a fox. How could she outwit him? She stepped back through the door as he came inside the hut carrying the bowl.

"My luggage," she said, raising her eyebrows.

"Anything my betrothed wishes," he said with a chuckle, holding out the bowl to her. When she took it, he dragged her bags inside the room but was out again as she moved toward the front door, planning to ditch the water and run.

"I wouldn't do that." He growled. "Don't make me angry."

Lucy silently went into the room and shut the door.

WITHOUT WASTING TIME, Hugh left London within the hour and took the road to Chigwell with Luke beside him. He refused to think of it as a wild goose chase. He wasn't about to give up until he found Lucy but admitted they had very little to go on. He didn't want to waste time putting up somewhere for the night, but the night was cloudy, and he had to consider the safety of his passenger and his horses.

"The clouds are blowing away," Luke said when Hugh had asked him what he thought. "I say we stop for dinner, water the horses, then go on."

Hugh nodded gratefully. "An excellent suggestion. Mrs. Grayswood's directions to the inn where she and Lucy spent the night will be helpful. Too much to expect the innkeeper to know of Rattray's direction, I suppose, but we'll stop there to dine and ask him a few questions."

Darkness fell as they reached the inn. It was a shabby establishment, and if they'd toyed with the idea of a meal, they quickly discounted it. Even the aromas from the kitchen didn't invite investigation. But the innkeeper was happy to talk about his recent guests and show them the bedchamber Mrs. Grayswood and Lucy had shared. It kept its secrets close, with no more than a delicate perfume lingering in the air. With a pang, Hugh recognized it as lily of the valley, Lucy's scent, which he'd found so appealing. Breathing it now sent a rush of anxiety flooding through him, along with the fierce urge to get back on the road in search of her. An inquiry of the stable staff was more enlightening. The groom had heard Rattray say to his coachman that he expected them to arrive at daybreak, or they wouldn't be paid. "They carried the girl into the coach, milord," the groom said with a sad shake of his head. "She seemed deeply asleep. I realized when morning came and the girl's aunt was so distraught that I should have done something to stop them, although they were armed. I did help the poor lady find a carriage to take her back to London."

Hugh wrestled down another bout of fear. He had to keep a clear mind. It wasn't time for speculation.

They were soon on the road again, the cool night wrapping around them. Would they be able to find Lucy in time?

"We'd best discuss how we'll go about this rescue," Luke said, showing remarkable confidence in their success. "It might be better if I handle Rattray, and you see to his servants, only two, according to the groom. By your expression, I fear you'll kill the fellow."

"Very likely," Hugh said through gritted teeth. "But allow me the pleasure of dealing with him."

Chapter Sixteen

T HERE WAS NO lock on the door. Lucy dragged the table over against it. It wouldn't keep Rattray out, but it would give her time to prepare herself. She washed her face and then her feet, drying them on a petticoat. Then, watching the door, she quickly stripped off her dressing gown and nightgown.

She drew on her shift and tied up her stays, then sat to pull on stockings. Donning her warmest gown, a lavender-gray wool with a high neck, she slipped into her half-boots. They would be best if she had to run through the forest. She'd left her hairpins on the dressing table at the inn and could only manage to brush and braid her hair. Then, feeling a little better, she peered into her reticule and withdrew a small notebook and pencil she carried. Resting it on her knee, she wrote about what had happened to her, what Rattray had done and said he would do, then slipped it into her stays. It appeared she was valuable to Rattray, so she doubted he'd kill her, not intentionally at least, not until after their marriage and he had the money. But should she die, she wanted whoever found her body to learn what he had done. She wanted her father to know what had happened to her and warn him that he was in danger of being suspected of murder. Hopefully, the note might be found. If Rattray told the truth and the marquess and both of his sons would die, her father would become the new marquess. But he would be left burdened with a heavy heart. She must try to escape.

The door opened and banged against the table. "What do you want?" she demanded.

"I have a roll for your breakfast."

"I don't want to eat it."

"But I insist."

It wouldn't suit him for her to die yet. But he wasn't above hurting her. At Rattray's hard shove, the table slid away, and he opened the door. "Come and sit by the fire. It's warmer there."

"I am perfectly comfortable here."

"Do as I say." He growled and came over to lean threateningly over her.

Lucy decided she'd have a better chance of escaping from out there and rose from the bed. She followed him through the door and took a seat on the ghastly sofa.

"Ahh, that's better." Rattray moved one of the chairs to sit closer. "I like to see your pretty face." He studied her while she stiffened with revulsion. "You've plaited your lovely hair. It's an invitation for a man to unravel it."

"Touch me, and I'll scratch your eyes out."

"My, my, such virulence. You're a spirited miss. I like that about you. I'm not about to seduce you. Not in this dirty place. It will be somewhere much more to my liking."

Her stomach turned over as she wondered where that was, and how long before they got there.

He rose and thrust a bun and a piece of cheese at her. "Eat."

Not wishing to anger him further, she took a bite. The bread stuck in her throat, making her gag. She coughed.

Rattray went over to his luggage and withdrew a glass bottle. "Drink some of this."

"I'm not so foolish," she said, pushing it away. "It will be drugged."

"It's not wine. It's cider. I don't want you unconscious."

She violently shook her head.

He removed the lid, raised the bottle and drank from it.

"Very well, please yourself." Then he went to stir the glowing embers in the fireplace.

Watching him, she thought her only chance might be to use the fire to set the hut alight. Then escape into the trees, where he couldn't find her. But he lit his pipe and settled back in the chair again. "We might as well be comfortable," he said. "We have hours to wait."

Hours to wait, and then what? Swallowing rising hysteria, Lucy saw the wooden box was empty, and the fire had died down. It was worth a try. "I'm cold." She shivered and rubbed her arms.

"If you ate something, you wouldn't be."

She shook her head sorrowfully. "I can't eat."

"There are logs right outside, so don't get any ideas," he said, going to the door.

She must act quickly, but there was nothing in the room that would suit her purpose. And there was little time. Lucy pulled her note from inside her stays, her original intention forgotten. She bent and thrust a corner of the page into the embers. Would her father know what happened to her should she not survive? But she wasn't going to die at that monster's hands if she could help it. When the paper caught, she cradled the fledgling flame with her hand and went to the thin fabric hanging at the window, which served as a curtain. Dry as dust, it caught quickly and went up with a *whoosh*.

She gleefully watched the flames, then went to the door. "We're on fire," she said cheerfully.

"You…" He cursed under his breath and raced to the pump. Filling a bowl which lay beside it, he ran inside. The flames ate greedily at the last of the fabric. Lucy, ready to run, edged out of his line of sight as he threw water at it.

Rattray swiveled and saw her and in a moment was on her. He backhanded her across the face. She fell to the floor. "Stay where you're put, vixen."

He took off his coat and fought the flames while she lay there, dizzy, her cheek smarting. Rattray finally got control, and the fire died to a smoky sizzle.

"Try anything again, and I won't guarantee you'll survive it," he said, shutting the front door. He came back to look down at her and offered his hand. "Now look what you made me do. Mar your pretty face."

Ignoring his offer of help, Lucy slowly climbed to her feet and walked toward the bedchamber.

"Yes, stay in there," he said, following her.

"You know, if my father is found to be guilty of murder, they will hang him," she said at the door. "And the next male in line will be marquess."

His eyes shone. "There is no one else in line. No one else at all, in fact. That would be true if it were only males who inherited. But in this case, rare as it might be, it is not. I have investigated the primogeniture laws applying to this title thoroughly. You would be coheiress and able to claim all the wealth and properties, if not the title, Lucy. Just think about that."

"What made you so evil?" she asked. "Were you born that way?"

His face reddened, and she saw with a burst of glee that she'd shaken him.

"I was born in a castle where my father worked his fingers to the bone while the laird ruled over us," he said furiously. "I vowed that one day, I would be the one who lived like a king and ordered people about. And you, shall be my entrée into that world."

"That is a foolish dream that will never come true!" She shut the door in his face and ran over to the bed. Throwing herself down, she gave way to tears. After a few minutes, she sniffed and wiped her eyes on a handkerchief. She mustn't sink into despair. It was vital to keep fighting and take advantage of anything that might present itself.

HUGH AND LUKE arrived in Chigwell as the moon rode high in the sky. Only two places were still open. Candlelight spilled out from the coaching inn and the Red Bull Tavern, which was farther along the road. Raucous laughter floated out of the tavern as Hugh went inside. Although it was late, there were still a few drinking ale and spirits and swapping stories. As he approached the tavern owner, who stood at the bar pouring drinks, a barmaid passed him with a tray. She cast him a saucy look as she moved among the tables, serving drinks and collecting empties.

Hugh ordered an ale. "Any strangers come in here during the last day or so?"

The proprietor paused and scratched at his ginger whiskers. "We get travelers in here quite regular like. Had a couple in early this morning looking for a meal. From London, they said. They've booked a room here for the night."

Hugh pulled a handful of coins from his pocket. "Hear anything they said?"

He eyed the money. "Ahh, let's see. Arrived in a coach. Coachman and groom, I'd say. The younger man deferred to the older one, and they discussed the condition of the horses. One horse needed shoeing. They planned on taking some gentleman and his lady north tomorra."

Hugh handed him the coins and held up one more. "Is the gentleman staying here too? Did you see him or the woman?"

The proprietor shook his head. "Didn't say where they was." He took the coin with a nod and turned back to remove tankards from the shelf. "That's all I can tell you. Try the inn."

Hugh nodded. "Thanks."

He went back out to Luke. "We've had a bit of luck. Looks like we might have found Rattray's coachman and groom. They're at the tavern and plan to put up there for the night. Leaving first thing in the morning to collect their client and his lady, so says the tavern owner. Rattray must have Lucy at the inn." He jumped in and drove the horses down the street. "I'll go and deal with Rattray while you drive around to the stables."

He was close to finding Lucy. He could feel it in his bones. But had Rattray ravished her? *Lucy!* He recoiled in horror. Why else would he go to all this trouble to snatch her away? And against her will. She'd told Hugh she didn't like him. Was the man madly in love with her? Men did stupid things for love, but Rattray didn't seem the type. Did he believe those irritating rumors about Lucy being an heiress? He should have acted to quash them before they'd spread. If Rattray had hurt one hair on Lucy's head, he would be swiftly dispatched from this world.

Hugh held out a coin as he questioned the innkeeper. But the man shook his untidy head of black hair. "Not staying here, they're not, milord."

Deeply disappointed, Hugh booked a room. As he and Luke went into the dining room, Hugh told his friend of his revised plan. "Rattray and Lucy must be staying somewhere in the area. We can grab a few hours' sleep and be up before cock's crow to follow their coach."

Luke yawned. "Sleep sounds irresistibly attractive."

In the inn bedchamber he shared with Luke, Hugh lay down and set his internal clock, something he'd mastered during his years in the army, to wake before dawn. And sure enough, he opened his eyes well before a glow lit the horizon.

He shook Luke's shoulder. "I'm awake," Luke said, and he leapt up from the bed.

"We'll put the horses in the traces and bring it around. Then have some coffee at the tavern while we wait for these men."

When their carriage was brought round, the tavern had opened its doors, and the enticing smells of frying bacon and coffee wafted out.

In the dining room, a large, gray-haired man with a rugged face and a lean, younger man with a weak one, sat eating eggs.

Hugh and Luke drank coffee and ate some toast, then paid

and went out to wait in the phaeton, a little way down the street

Not long afterward, the men's shabby coach rattled around the corner from the rear of the stables and took off down the street.

Hugh urged the horses into a trot, and they followed the coach at a discreet distance.

The coachman turned off onto a rutted track and the badly sprung vehicle careened down it. Hugh still followed at a distance. He pulled the horses up before the bend, and he and Luke continued on foot.

The track ended at a rudimentary timber hunting lodge, with the coach waiting outside, the door to the hut open.

Rattray could be seen ordering Lucy to move. She looked scared and exhausted and was dragging her feet.

"Remember when you said I should tackle the servants and you would get Rattray?" Hugh whispered.

"Yes."

"Forget it. I'll go in and deal with Rattray," he said grimly. "The coachman and the groom might choose not to get involved."

Luke took out his pistol. "I'll have a pleasant chat with them."

Hugh intended to give Luke a few minutes to make sure they didn't kick up a fuss, but the rogues jumped up onto the box and turned the coach around, rattling away down the track.

"I'll make sure they leave," Luke yelled, bolting down the track in pursuit.

Rattray appeared at the door. "What in hell?"

"Good morning, Rattray," Hugh said, brandishing his pistol. "Shall we talk inside?"

"Why the devil are you here, Dorchester? This isn't your affair."

"Abducting a lady? I think you'll find it is."

"You are interfering in an elopement."

Hugh nudged Rattray back into the room.

"Hugh!" Lucy stood pale and still, her eyes wide. A bruise

darkened her cheek and another on her chin, and there were deep, violet half-moons beneath her eyes.

"You villain!" Hugh punched Rattray in the solar plexus and as the cretin staggered back with an *"oomph,"* Hugh dealt him a brutal left undercut to his jaw, then followed it up with a stinging right. Rattray folded up like a fan and fell, then lay spread-eagled on the floor, cursing in a very ungentlemanly like manner, while feeling his jaw.

His eye on Rattray, Hugh went to Lucy, wanting to make sure she was unhurt. "Did this villain harm you?"

She put her hand to her cheek. "No. Only bruises."

"I'll be with you in a moment, sweetheart."

Lying on the floor, Rattray watched him keenly, like a snake watches its prey.

Hugh brandished his pistol. "Get up. We'll see what the magistrate makes of this."

"You won't shoot me," Rattray said. "You lords are too soft and lily-livered." He reached down and pulled a small pistol from his boot, and as his finger tightened on the trigger, Hugh flung himself to the side. As the bullet hit the wall behind him, Hugh fired.

Rattray stumbled back, clutching his chest, where blood had begun to seep through his waistcoat. He crumpled to the floor with a gurgling sound, his head falling back.

Hugh kneeled beside him, but it was clear the man was dead.

At the sound of the shots, Luke ran inside. "What the...?" He bent over to the prostrate man. "Dead. Pity, I would have liked to spend some time with the villain."

Lucy stood with her hands over her ears. Then, with a gasp at the dead body, she ran into Hugh's arms.

Hugh had gathered Lucy's trembling body close and shielded her from the sight. "You're safe now, sweetheart." He glanced at the burned curtain. "It looks like you've been giving him some trouble."

"I tried to burn the hut down," she murmured, clutching his

coat. "But I'm afraid it didn't work. I'm so glad to see you and Mr. Beaufort." With a shuddering gasp, she drew away. "Rattray admitted he was responsible for poisoning the Marquess of Berwick and his sons. He claims one child died, even."

Hugh hadn't shot a man since the war and had hoped never to do so again. He shook his head. *Dear Lord. The man was mad.*"

"Poor Aunt Mary was completely taken in by him," Lucy said. Her eyes widened. "Aunt Mary must have told you he'd taken me."

"Yes. She came back to London the next morning to ask for Sarah's help."

"Is she all right?"

"Somewhat unnerved by the experience, but when she sees you, I'm sure she'll be much better." He gazed tenderly down at her. "We'll go back into Chigwell and see the parish constable. Shouldn't be a matter for the magistrate, not with a witness to the fact that Rattray fired first." His bullet had shattered a timber panel on the wall.

"I'll testify I saw that as well," Luke said.

"No." Lucy put her hand to her cheek. "I shan't have you lie for me. No more lies. My witness testimony will surely be enough."

"Right." Luke bent to drag the body outside.

"Better to leave it as it is, Luke," Hugh said. "And his gun. The constable will want to view the scene."

Luke nodded and went outside to bring the phaeton closer to the house.

Hugh raised Lucy's tear-stained face and gazed tenderly into her eyes, hating to see how she'd suffered at that scoundrel's hands. He couldn't help himself. He kissed her, her lips as soft and sweet as they were in his dreams.

"I've wanted to tell you how I felt for weeks," he admitted when he drew away. "But I wasn't free. I had an unresolved betrothal to deal with."

"And now?" she asked searching his eyes.

"Miss Ashton is to marry someone else."

"Hugh," she murmured as her arms slid around his neck, and she pressed herself against him. His hands at her waist, he pressed his mouth to hers again as blood raced through his veins. It was all he could do to end the kiss and pull away. His heart banged in his chest at his palpable relief. He'd been grinding his jaw since he'd first heard of her abduction, and a muscle jumped.

"How on Earth did you find me?"

Lucy looked dirty, bruised, and bewildered, which stirred a fierce desire in him to protect her. To never let her suffer harm again.

"Time for all that later." At the profound relief, he wanted to hold her in his arms. Hugh tried to ignore his emotional turmoil as he gathered up her bonnet, pelisse, and reticule. "We'll stay at the inn in Chigwell tonight," he said as he helped her into her pelisse.

Once her bonnet was on her head and she clutched her reticule, he swept her up into his arms and strode with her to the phaeton. Luke followed and climbed in behind, and Hugh drove them the short distance to the village inn.

Hugh booked two rooms, saw Lucy into one, then went to see to the horses.

Luke came back within the hour with the constable, Mr. Riley, a short, stocky gentleman with an earnest face. Not long afterward, Lucy came down having refreshed herself, and backed up Hugh's account that Rattray had fired first, as well as everything she knew about the man's crimes. The villainy of which seemed to shock Mr. Riley, who appeared convinced it had been self-defense. But he would examine the hut for evidence and have the body removed. He'd return if there were any questions.

Hugh ordered luncheon, and they sat in the inn's dining room while he explained how they'd come to find her. "It was fortunate we found the coachman and the groom at the tavern, for we had little to go on."

"I'm so glad my aunt is safe," Lucy said, placing a hand over her mouth as she yawned.

"Up to bed with you, as soon as you've eaten," he said.

Lucy didn't argue. "I can't thank you both enough," she said passionately.

"I'm sure to be in Lady Sarah's bad books, as I canceled an invitation to take her to see the celebrations in Hyde Park," Luke said at the end of the meal. He grinned and rose. "I'll hire a horse from the stables down the road and ride back to London. I need to visit her and apologize. See you there, Hugh."

Hugh stood to shake his hand. "You've been a good friend, and indispensable, Luke. If you require me to put in a good word with Sarah, you have only to ask me." He grinned. "Although coming from me, it can sometimes prove unhelpful." He fervently hoped Luke would one day become part of the family. If any man could drive Viscount Cardew out of Sarah's mind and heart, it would be Luke.

Hugh saw Lucy to her chamber. "I must tell you the rest of it, that which I failed to tell the constable because I didn't want my father drawn into it. The evil things Rattray has done and what he planned to do," she said as she stood at the door.

"All in good time." He framed her face in his hands examined her bruised face, then he dropped a light kiss on her lips. "Shall I send for a doctor?"

"No, I don't need one."

He opened the door for her. "We'll leave for London first thing tomorrow."

She put up a hand to trace his chin with a finger, sending a flood of warmth straight to his groin. "Tomorrow, then."

"I'll fetch your luggage in the morning, before breakfast. Can you manage without it tonight?"

"Of course." She pushed an errant wisp out of her eyes. "Clothes are of no consequence."

He shook his head and smiled, briskly banishing the vision of her sleeping naked, which did nothing to help the discomfort in his breeches, then retreated hastily downstairs. Tonight after dinner, he'd play cards at the tavern to resist calling in to see how she fared.

Chapter Seventeen

IN BED, LUCY dwelled on Hugh's kisses. Her toes curled, remembering how he'd looked at her. The flame of passion in his eyes. Would he kiss her again? If he'd come into the bedchamber, she wouldn't have resisted him. She was shameless where Hugh was concerned.

At the knock at the door, Lucy woke with a start. The sun crept in through gaps in the curtains. It must have been late! Was it Hugh?

She leapt from the bed, then realized with panic that she only wore her shift. "Please wait," she called, then she threw her dress over her head and rushed to the door.

The boot boy stood there with her luggage. She thanked him as he carried it over to the bed. Hugh must have gone to the hut this morning very early to fetch it. She went limp with relief, recognizing she would never have to see the place again. Then she busied herself, sorting through her clothes and selected her crushed traveling gown.

A wave of compassion gripped her. *Poor Aunt Mary.* She had told Lucy to pack an evening gown. Her aunt had imagined they would be dining in elegant splendor with that rogue!

Suddenly ravenous, Lucy stripped and poured cold water into a bowl at the washstand. Shivering, she washed herself, wincing when she gently washed her face. The view in the mirror shocked her. Her hair had unraveled from its plait, wisps hanging down around her face like an eagle's nest. How dreadful she looked with her bruised face, but the deep relief and the fledgling joy she allowed herself made her appearance seem less important. She dressed quickly, sighing over her torn stockings. There was little she could do with her curls except tie them back with a ribbon.

Lucy slipped on her shoes. How brave Hugh was. How masterful! When he'd run into the hut and found her, his gaze so concerned, her heart had turned over, despite being terrified for his safety. But in the end, Rattray had been no match for him.

Hugh had come all this way to save her. It was difficult to grasp that after everything that had happened, her future had changed for the better. Would their path to matrimony run smooth, or would something else happen to prevent it? *"Oh, stop!"* With a last glance in the mirror, she went downstairs, eager to see him. She wanted to grasp at happiness now, with both hands.

He waited in the foyer, his eyes tender as he greeted her. He had shaved and smelled of soap. Elegant and handsome, he made her heart leap.

Over breakfast, he told her what he'd discovered about her cousin Anabel.

"You think she might really be in Ireland?" Lucy asked, hopeful for her aunt's sake.

"It seems likely they would go first to his family. At least until they make plans. That is, unless…"

She knew what he wouldn't say. That their relationship might not have survived the pressures that would have been brought to bear on them both. Once alone, would their love remain strong? Would his family accept her after the divorce? Would Anabel be happy living such a different life away from her family? Lucy hoped so.

After breakfast, Lucy packed her few things into the portmanteau. At the knock on the door, she expected the boot boy to take down her luggage. But when she opened it, Hugh stood there with such warmth and longing in his eyes. Lucy reached up and grabbed his coat.

He stepped into the room and put his arms around her, his head resting against hers and his breath stirring the curls at her neck. "I should not be here," he murmured, straightening to gaze at her, "I must tell you…"

She reached up to touch his cheek. "You can tell me all of it, later, Hugh. I want you to take me to bed."

"Lucy," he groaned, his hands on her shoulders holding her at a distance. "I shouldn't be here with you, without a chaperone," he said with a laugh. "I have hopes that I will soon be free to come to you, to claim you, sweetheart. But we must wait a little while yet. Not until Miss Ashton is married and leaves England. I promised her father."

"Who is Miss Ashton to marry?" Surely, she hadn't found anyone as wonderful as Hugh.

"Our vicar, Mr. Benson."

Instead of an earl? "Will her parents agree?"

"Isabel is with child. It is necessary to be discreet until she and her vicar sail for Ceylon."

Lucy's eyes widened. "A child? Ceylon? Heavens. Well, I wish them well." What a good man Hugh was. He didn't seem angry about Miss Ashton's actions at all. She coiled her arms around his neck. "Kiss me, Hugh."

She leaned against him, feeling his strength and the hardness of his body. He brushed his lips against hers, then captured her mouth in a long, passionate kiss. When he broke away, she moaned and reached up to stroke his hair back from his forehead. "You don't want me?"

"Want you? With every breath I take," he said, his voice low. At the passionate plea in her eyes, he took her hand and led her over to the bed.

Lucy's breath quickened, and she sat quickly before her knees gave way. Her heart beat madly and her fingers ached to touch him.

"You don't wish to be chaste at your wedding? Everyone will assume you are. It will be a lie."

"This lie doesn't matter, Hugh."

He joined her on the bed, his muscular arms and fresh cologne enveloping her, as he pressed kisses along the sensitive skin beneath her ear.

Lucy's breasts tingled.

Hugh's hands shaped her breasts through her gown, his thumbs stroking her nipples into hard peaks. "You are so very lovely, Lucy."

She closed her eyes at the wonderful feeling, pleased that he thought so. "Shall I take off my gown?"

"No, sweetheart. As much as I'd enjoy it, I won't risk it. I want you too much."

She was offering herself to him, and he rejected her? Did he not truly desire her?

A glance at her expression must have told him of her feelings. "Lucy, I think we should wait. I shall have that pleasure on our honeymoon."

She sighed, but she had to agree with him. She was terribly inexperienced in these matters.

"Lucy," he murmured as he rested his hands on each side of her head, then bent and claimed her mouth in a long, passionate kiss.

She stroked her hands over his shoulders, rendered slightly dizzy by the strength and warmth of his hard body.

He eased away and untied the strings on her gown. Then he pulled the bodice and her stays down to uncover her thin shift, revealing the thrust of her breasts and pink nipples beneath. He cupped a breast, while he kissed the pulsing hollow at the base of her throat, then trailed hot kisses down to circle a nipple through the thin lawn. Her thoughts fragmented as he tended to the other breast, while tweaking the first with his fingers.

She moaned and lay back with abandon, unable to think of anything but him and how he was making her feel.

He eased himself over her and when his mouth covered hers, she arched against him. When his hard erection pressed against her, Lucy was gripped by a powerful need. She moaned, wanting to feel that part of him and for him to touch her in that special place. She wanted to experience everything, knowing he would be gentle. That she could trust him.

He stroked his hand up her stocking to the warm flesh of her thigh. Her cheeks burned, and she stilled, as he touched the sensitive soft folds at her center. It felt extraordinary, and so right, that she closed her eyes. "Yes," she murmured.

He bent to kiss her inner thigh as he touched her there. At the exquisite friction his stroking caused, she clutched at his silky hair, embarrassed by the slick sound of her damp flesh, and the aroma of her arousal.

Hugh groaned. He slipped a finger a little way inside her while he plundered her mouth. The sensation of his tongue stroking inside her mouth mimicked his touch. Lucy feared she would lose all sense of herself. A powerful throb at her core made her whimper, and she cried out, riding waves of intense feeling. When it finally eased away, she fell back against the pillow.

Hugh rose quickly and turned away, but not before she saw the evidence of his desire tenting his breeches. She still craved more. More of him. To lie naked against him and discover all of his body, the muscles, bones, and tendons, so different from her own. And that part of her she had never seen. But she knew that no matter how aroused he was, Hugh would not give in to her demands.

After adjusting his breeches, he returned to her. "Come, sweetheart," he said, his voice gruff. He bent and pressed a lingering kiss on her lips. "Time to drive back to London. I'll ask the innkeeper if a widow in the town might agree to chaperone you."

Lucy wrinkled her nose. "If you must, Hugh." She rose, her legs trembling, her senses sharply alive, still patently aware of his masculine smell and how his deft touch had brought about her very first experience of passion, and the pleasure lovers could give each other. But it wasn't enough, not nearly enough. Her dreams were about to come true, and because she'd been through so much to come to this, she feared it would all come to an end. That she would wake up and find it was, after all, a dream.

HUGH REGAINED HIS breath and the discomfort in his trousers eased as they went downstairs. He could have taken her to bed. Lucy wouldn't have stopped him. And she would not have rebuked him later, as she had the kind of bedrock honesty beneath everything she did, and took responsibility for her own actions. But he would have been taking advantage of her. She had suffered from Rattray's villainy and was weak and exhausted. She was not thinking clearly, and he wanted her desperately. But what he wanted uppermost was to take care of her.

The next morning, they left the village and he drove the carriage onto the road to London with Mrs. Bromley, who had accepted the position as chaperone. The stern-faced widow sat behind them in silence after taking out her knitting. Hugh gazed at his lovely bride-to-be beside him, who narrowed her eyes at him. Earlier, she had made no secret that she didn't want a chaperone. He chuckled. "It's a long journey to undertake in one day, but I don't plan to stop again. It will be late when we reach London."

Mrs. Bromley made no complaint. She planned to spend a few days with her sister in Cheapside.

When Lucy had told him and the constable about what Rattray had done to the Marquess of Berwick in Carlisle, he'd been furious. And he was doubly glad the man was no longer able to hurt her, or anyone else. If only he'd told Lucy about Baron Maitland sooner. It would surely have been enough for her aunt to refuse Rattray's offer of a jaunt to the country.

"I shall write to the laird and tell him the news," he said looking down at Lucy, who gravely nodded.

The horses settled into a rhythm and the carriage traveled smoothly over the road. Hugh smiled at Lucy and put an arm around her. She rested her head against his shoulder.

Chapter Eighteen

A s Lucy leaned against Hugh's powerful body, she longed for when they could be together alone as husband and wife. Hugh was determined to undertake the journey in one day. Lucy had hoped to spend another night at an inn with him. Then perhaps... She put her fingers to her lips, surprised at how bold she'd become.

Hugh's face looked thoughtful in the shadow of his beaver hat. She would have liked to ask him if he'd enjoyed what they had shared. But with Mrs. Bromley's disapproving silence behind her, she couldn't.

The horses responded well to his hands on the reins. He seemed so calm and confident in everything he did. She wanted to lean against him, for some of his warmth and strength to seep into her tired bones, but apart from her thinking it too presumptuous, she feared she'd fall asleep.

As if reading her mind, Hugh's strong arm settled her against him. "Rest, sweetheart," he said, his deep voice rumbling in his chest where she lay her head.

A glance behind her told her Mrs. Bromley had fallen asleep, her knitting on her lap, her bonnet pushed down over her eyes.

Lucy had never felt so safe. She closed her heavy lids, and at the soporific effect caused by the pounding rhythm of the thoroughbreds, she too, slept.

She woke to darkness when they reached London, and the gas lamps lit up the darkness in Pall Mall.

When Hugh helped her down outside her aunt's house, Lucy hurried inside with him, eager to tell her aunt about Anabel. The thought went immediately out of her head when Aunt Mary, in sad disarray, her shawl askew and wearing only one earring, which was so unlike her, almost stumbled across the drawing room carpet to fling herself into Lucy's arms, with a burst of loud sobbing. "I thought I'd lost you. How could I ever tell your father?" she wailed.

Lucy felt a little guilty. Somehow, Rattray had faded from her mind, banished by Hugh's kisses. She hoped what had happened between them wasn't evident on her face. "I am perfectly well, Aunt, really. When Rattray tried to shoot Lord Dorchester, the earl shot and killed him."

Her aunt drew in a sharp breath. "The villain! Lord Dorchester, how can I ever thank you?" She croaked, swiveling to Hugh. She dabbed her eyes with a sodden handkerchief.

"It's entirely unnecessary, Mrs. Grayswood. My reward is to bring Miss Kershaw home safe."

Aunt Mary stared at him for a moment, then turned back to Lucy, whose arm she still held as if Lucy might vanish into thin air. "I am *so* sorry, my dear. What a fool I was to be taken in by Rattray."

"He deceived a lot of people," Hugh said.

"Where are my manners? Please sit, my lord. Allow me to order you a libation. You must be parched."

"Thank you, I must go. Miss Kershaw's chaperone, Mrs. Bromley, is in the carriage. I'm to take her to her sister's house in Cheapside. And I mustn't leave my tired horses standing."

"Oh, yes, of course. You've had a long journey."

Hugh smiled. "No need to see me out." He turned to Lucy. "I'll call in a day or so, Miss Kershaw."

After Lucy returned to the drawing room, Aunt Mary drew her over to the sofa. "Your face is bruised! Did that scoundrel

Rattray hurt you?" Her anxious gaze roamed Lucy's face. "I was so afraid he would—"

The thought of Rattray forcing himself on her made Lucy's stomach lurch. "No. He didn't. The horrid man intended to take me to Scotland and marry me there. Lord Dorchester and Mr. Beaufort arrived in time to stop him from driving away with me in his carriage."

"Wed you? In Scotland?" Aunt Mary cried, looking horrified. "What a duplicitous rogue!" She shook her head. "What a fool I was... I had thought..."

"He gave you good reason to believe it, Aunt Mary. He was very cunning."

"Indeed, he was. But you saw through him, didn't you, Lucy?"

"I didn't like him, that's true. But I certainly never suspected him capable of such evil."

Lucy still trembled, thinking about how Rattray had planned to hurt her father. But that was at an end, she reminded herself. The man was dead. She shivered and shoved away the grim image of his body lying, bleeding, at her feet. "He planned for us to marry because he knew, if the marquess and his sons died, Papa would inherit the title and estate."

Her aunt looked startled. "That's what I wished to tell you. News has reached London from Carlisle. Berwick's two sons have died, poisoned, it's said. But the marquess still clings to life."

"Dear heavens!" Lucy put her hands to her mouth as her chest tightened, robbing her of breath. "Rattray was a murderer of children!" she gasped out. "He confessed to me that he was responsible for their deaths."

Aunt Mary looked confused. "But how could he be, when he was here with us?"

"He paid a servant to poison the house's water." Lucy rubbed her eyes. She wanted to sleep for a week. "When I've rested, Aunt, I'll tell you all of it."

"Yes, of course." Aunt Mary jumped up. She chewed her lip

and fretted, as if eager to forget what Lucy had just said. "You're exhausted, my dear. After you've had your supper, you shall go straight to bed."

Lucy stretched. "I would love a bath." She wanted to wash away all traces of Rattray's hands on her.

Her aunt rose. "Of course. I'll order Maisie to bring up the hip bath and hot water to your bedchamber."

"Oh, Aunt, I must tell you! Lord Dorchester believes he has discovered where Anabel has gone."

"His lordship knows where she is?" Her aunt shook her head, as though she struggled to believe it. "How? Where is she?"

"It's not certain, but Mr. Connor has family in Killarney. Hugh believes that's where he would have taken Anabel."

"Then I must undertake the journey to Ireland to find her." Aunt Mary straightened her back. At the door, she turned to Lucy. "You called the earl 'Hugh.'" She frowned. "Lucy, I know you are grateful to him, but he is a betrothed man."

"I shouldn't, I know," Lucy said, feeling she couldn't tell her aunt more until Hugh returned. "But I have grown so fond of him." But she wanted an end to secrecy and lies. And once they were married, she was determined to be a proper lady.

"Oh, my dear, of course you have." She patted Lucy's hand. "We are both very grateful to him. And I suppose for him to go all that way to rescue you, one must think he cares for your welfare. But don't expect too much, Lucy." She went to ring the bell. "Now for your bath and your supper." Lucy smiled and hugged her secret to herself for just a little longer, before it became known. What would the *ton* make of it?

Relaxed after her supper and the bath, Lucy settled down in bed. She went over everything that had happened in her mind. She wriggled with pleasure at what had occurred between Hugh and her in the inn bedchamber. Hugh's kisses… He was muscular and strong and yet his hands were gentle. She loved his masculine smell. How silky his dark hair had felt sliding through her fingers.

Lucy sighed and thumped her pillow. Lucy would never tell a

soul about Miss Ashton. It meant such a lot to her that Hugh desired her instead, and trusted her with his secrets. How he looked at her! The soft light of love in his eyes made her sink back and sigh. She groaned. She wished that this hadn't come to mind. Now she would never be able to rest. But, surprisingly, as soon as she closed her eyes, Morpheus, the god of sleep, claimed her.

As soon as Hugh walked into the house, Sarah ran to meet him. "You didn't tell Mama or me where you were going," she accused him.

He took his mail from the silver salver in the entry hall. "Must I tell you everything?" He eyed her, suddenly worried. "Is Mama ill again?"

"*Au contraire*, she's dressing to go to a dinner party. She will be pleased to see you."

"That's good news. She must be feeling better. It's just you and I for this evening, then. How about a game of chess?"

Sarah grinned. "Yes, please." As he walked to the library for a brandy, she called him back. "I thought I'd ask Lucy to ride with me tomorrow. I'm sure Mr. Beaufort will join us if you come too."

"Leave it for a few days, will you, Sarah? I'm a little weary."

She narrowed her eyes. "You can be out until dawn and are never too tired to ride. I don't believe you, but there's no point in me attempting to find out where you've been."

"How do you know when I'm out until dawn? You are worse than the Spanish Inquisition." Hugh laughed. "But I'm pleased you've come to accept that you can't pry too much into a fellow's activities, Sarah. Or you'll make a most annoying wife for someone."

"Was Mr. Beaufort with you?"

Amused, he raised a casual eyebrow. "Why do you ask?"

"He canceled our engagement. He was to accompany me to Hyde Park to see the Great Fair to celebrate the Allied sovereigns' visit to England. There are stalls and shows, and the Battle of Trafalgar is to be reenacted on the Serpentine. I was very disappointed, and I found his excuse rather vague. If I didn't know better, I'd think he'd lost interest in me."

By her expression, she was obviously upset. As Luke had spoken of little else but Sarah on their journey north, it was clear that he'd missed her, and his feelings had not changed one iota. Hugh held her shoulders. "That is definitely not the case, Sarah. Luke was away from London. He assisted me when Lucy was kidnapped by her aunt's friend, Mr. Rattray."

Sarah gasped. "Poor Lucy! Tell me more, Hugh!"

"Rattray took Lucy to a hut near Epping Forest," Hugh said. "Luke and I were able to rescue her. I'm not about to explain it all to you. Lucy can if she wishes."

Sarah put her hands to her face. "But that's horrible. Is Lucy all right?"

"Yes, she appears to have recovered well from her ordeal."

Sarah twisted the cameo ring on her finger, her eyes distraught. "I must go and see her."

"Of course. But not for a few days, Sarah. She is very tired."

"What did that nasty individual want with her?"

"He had some absurd plan to marry her and benefit financially from her father's inheritance." He shrugged. "Completely mad."

"How terrifying for Lucy." Sarah gasped. "Oh, I forgot, Hugh. I am sorry."

Hugh turned back to her again, with a heavy sigh. "For what, Sarah?"

"Tomorrow is Saturday. The day of Miss Ashton's wedding."

He smiled. "I hadn't forgotten. I'll see you at dinner."

Hugh entered the library and shut the door. The candles were ablaze, and a small fire had been lit waiting his return. He went to the drinks tray, poured a glass of brandy, and took his favorite wing chair. Stretching his legs out toward the heat, he wondered how Lucy fared after the nightmare Rattray had inflicted on her. She was stronger than she looked, thank God. And after tomorrow, he planned to see the couple off at the docks on Sunday. If they were there. Because the wedding was held in Canterbury, and he'd been advised not to attend it, he had hoped to receive a letter of confirmation from Sir Phillip. If things went as he hoped, he would invite Lucy to join them in Hyde Park at the Great Fair, where they could speak of their wedding and the future. He knew they would be happy together. There had always been something strong between them. It wasn't merely attraction, or desire he felt, although there was certainly that. Whenever they were together, it felt so right to be with her. Was it foolish to believe she was his soul mate? Yet he believed it so. He needed a lifetime to discover all those things about Lucy he did not yet know. To love her and have the absolute pleasure in making her happy. Once they were betrothed, he would quash any rumors about Lucy before they hurt his mother and sister.

When he sifted through his mail, he found a letter from Isabel. Slightly unnerved, he snatched up the letter opener from his desk. Slitting the paper, he read it while standing.

Isabel wrote that her father had suffered a change of heart. Hugh tensed and read on. Sir Phillip had offered Isabel an alternative. She could go away into the country with her mother until the birth. A good home would be found for the babe. Then she would return and enjoy life as a free woman. Isabel's tears smudged the page. *As if I could part with my baby! But we can't be married without Papa's consent,* she wrote. Smudged ink spots blotted the page. *I am underage, as you know. I remain hopeful Papa will support us. Should Michael and I marry as planned, we will set sail from London docks the following day, Sunday, on the evening tide. If you could come and see us off, we would love to see you.*

Hugh groaned, profoundly sorry for Isabel as he sat in the chair, his drink untouched. Might Lady Ashton hold out some hope he and Isabel would still marry in the future? If so, she would be disappointed and should instead allow her daughter to marry the man she loves. As would he. Hugh firmed his jaw. There was no way he'd allow anyone to stand between him and Lucy. He'd go to the docks on Sunday to see if Isabel and Mr. Benson were about to sail. He'd wave them off to their new life with the hope that it would treat Isabel well.

The door opened and his mother peeked in. "Well, here you are at last, Hugh. Where have you been?"

"It's a long story, Mama."

She stepped inside and he saw she was dressed in a lavender evening gown with diamonds at her throat. "Tell me tomorrow. I am dining with the Constables."

He smiled, delighted with how much brighter she seemed. "You look ravishing."

She laughed. "Every woman should have a son to compliment her."

The door closed again and left Hugh with his uneasy thoughts.

Chapter Nineteen

Lucy hoped to see Hugh on Sunday, but he didn't come. On Monday, she roamed the house, until her aunt grew annoyed with her and urged her to sit down and write to her father. Lucy had put off writing to him. Every time she'd begun, the story of her abduction sounded so alarming, no matter how she phrased it, she feared he would be dreadfully upset. He might demand she come back immediately from this iniquitous city to the safety of Bath. And she just couldn't leave now.

She was scratching out a letter in the parlor when the front door knocker sounded. William went to answer the door. She sat up and waited. Then she heard the deep voice she longed to hear.

She was on her feet when William showed him in. A little fearful of what he might tell her, she tried to gauge it from his expression, but his face gave her no clue. "Won't you please sit down, Lord Dorchester?"

Hugh shook his head with a smile and came to take her hands. "Are we back to using formal address again?"

Her knees trembled, but she managed to frown at him. Was he teasing her? Had he told his mother? Would her lie make her unacceptable to his family? Would it soon be over between them? She wished he would tell her.

Hugh urged her to sit on the sofa and joined her there. He turned toward her. "I went to the docks yesterday to see if Isabel and her new husband were there ready to depart on a ship bound for Ceylon."

"And were they?" she asked impatiently as she searched his eyes for an answer.

"Yes. Isabel got her way in the end, as she threatened to create a scandal by returning to live in the parish with Benson. I gave them a basket of fruit from our hothouses to eat onboard and stayed to watch them sail."

Lucy released the breath. "I wish them a safe voyage."

"As do I. I feared for Isabel's health and told them I thought it unwise for her to travel." A smile pulled at his lips. "Of course they took no notice of me. Do lovers ever listen to sound advice?"

While he spoke, his eyes sent a very different message. Lucy swallowed and licked her bottom lip.

Hugh put his arms around her. He palmed her chin and pressed a kiss on her lips. "I meant to court you, my love. To give you my grandmother's ring, which is still in the bank. But I find myself unable to wait."

Her heart beat so fast, she thought she'd faint.

"Will you marry me, Lucy?" he asked. He smiled, but his voice sounded strained. "As soon as is humanly possible?"

"Of course I will, my darling." She reached up to touch his face. "Kiss me again."

They broke apart at the sound of her aunt's footsteps on the stairs. Hugh moved to put some distance between them on the sofa. "It seems the only way to keep you out of trouble," he added with a rueful smile.

"Oh!" Lucy laughed. "Hugh, you are a disgraceful tease."

Aunt Mary came in, her eyes wide with shock. "Lucy. My lord, please forgive my niece's deplorable manners. She is overcome with her ordeal."

Hugh stood and went to greet her. "Lucy has agreed to become my wife, Mrs. Grayswood. I hope you will give us your blessing."

"Oh, my goodness!" her aunt cried. Throwing etiquette to

the winds, she left him and rushed over to hug Lucy. "This is wonderful news." Making a concerted effort to calm herself, she turned back to Hugh, who stood abandoned and amused. "My lord, forgive me. I am overcome. This is so unexpected. Especially, after all we have been through, and I cannot thank you enough for rescuing Lucy, and finding out where I might find my daughter Anabel ..." Scarlet-faced, she looked helpless, having run out of words.

"Thank you for your blessing, Mrs. Grayswood," Hugh said. "I must go, but I shall call again later today for a drive to the park. Lucy and I can discuss the future."

Aunt Mary nodded, still dazed.

Lucy rose and went to place a hand on his arm. She smiled up at him. "I'll see you to the door."

In the hall, she went to open the front door, but he drew her back into his arms. "I am impatient, Miss Kershaw."

"As am I, my lord?"

Hugh kissed her again.

Lucy stood with him in the street. She threaded her arms around his neck. "Let the whole world see," she murmured as he pulled her close. "I don't care."

He pulled away after a kiss, which made them both breathless. "I believe you will lead me a merry dance, Miss Kershaw."

"I hope to," she admitted.

"And you no longer worry about the rumors?"

For a moment, the fear of scandal hovered. Then she breathed a sigh. "It appears that Mrs. Vellacott will just have to come to accept the rumor as truth," she said slowly, her eyes sad.

"The news from Carlisle of Lord Berwick isn't encouraging," Hugh said. "Suffering the recent loss of his wife and now his sons, he would be in very low spirits."

"I am so sorry for him. I'll pray his lordship survives. I was in the process of writing to Papa. But I now have so much more to put in my letter," she said. "He will be thrilled to learn of our betrothal."

"I will drive to Bath as soon as I can to ask his permission." He smiled. "Will he forgive me for my lack of manners?"

Happy tears filled her eyes. "Of course. Papa will be over-joyed that I am marrying such a pillar of society. How could he not be?"

Hugh laughed. "You make me sound very stuffy." Hugh wiped the tears gently away with a finger. He gathered her to him, and his kiss was not like what one would expect from a pillar of society. "Sarah will be thrilled and my mother too. I will relay our news to them when I reach home. Tomorrow, I'll take you to see them." At the curricle, he turned back with a grin. "In the meantime, expect a visit from my sister at any moment."

Lucy smiled, suspecting he was right as she watched him drive away. Then she went in to talk to her aunt about the coming nuptials. She imagined Aunt Mary, who hoped Hugh could help her, was still too concerned about Anabel and the ensuing scandal to think of grandiose ideas concerning the ceremony and wedding breakfast. Lucy couldn't be sure and must remain firm. Hugh expressed the desire for quick nuptials. And with her father planning to go to Carlisle, she would prefer a small, quiet wedding. But Hugh was an earl, and she was very conscious of his position in society. His wishes on the subject were paramount.

As Hugh predicted, Sarah arrived within the hour. She rushed in to throw her arms around Lucy. "Have you recovered from your ordeal? How awful it must have been! Were you very frightened?"

"Yes. I was at the time. There's so much to think about now, I seldom dwell on it."

"I've wanted you for my sister-in-law, since we first met," Sarah confessed, sitting beside Lucy on the sofa. "And I must admit to working to that end, because I saw how attracted Hugh was to you. I like Miss Ashton—Mrs. Benson. We saw a lot of each other growing up in neighboring estates, but I always thought for them to marry would be a mistake. They were never more than friends." She smiled. "Now tell me everything, before I tell you my news. I'll give you a clue," she said with a mischievous smile. "Another of our family could be about to get married."

Lucy stared at her. "You and Mr. Beaufort?"

Sarah shook her head. "He has asked to court me." She giggled. "He kisses divinely."

Lucy grinned. "When did this happen?"

"In the garden at the Feldman's rout. Behind a hedge. There was a fountain tinkling in the background." Sarah sighed. "It was very romantic."

"It must have been," Lucy said delighted for her.

"And I have other news! Mama has a new suitor! Viscount Forester. Apparently, they met again during a dinner last week and renewed their friendship. A widower, he was a good friend of Papa's." Sarah laughed.

Delighted, Lucy laughed. "That is wonderful news!"

Sarah's eyes sparkled. "The doctor says that Mama's health is no longer a concern. She is now turning her attention to your wedding and wishes to visit your aunt."

"Aunt Mary will be thrilled," Lucy said. But would Hugh accept the lavish wedding they might plan for them? She rather doubted it.

"I QUITE LIKE Miss Kershaw," Hugh's mother said in the morning room. "Sarah considers her a good friend. She seems to have a good head on her shoulders. But I know nothing of her family."

Hugh stretched out his legs over the rug. "Lucy's father resides in Bath. Should the ailing Marquess of Berwick pass away before Mr. Kershaw does, he will inherit the title."

"Yes, I read of that sad occurrence in the newspaper. Berwick has lost his two sons. How tragic." She reached up to stroke

Hugh's cheek. "Well, it appears change is coming for all of us. I suspect Sarah and Mr. Beaufort's marriage will soon follow."

"It appears likely. I must admit I couldn't wish for better for Sarah. Luke is an excellent fellow."

His mother gazed at him wryly. "You must be pleased, as you brought it about."

Hugh raised his eyebrows. "Mama! How could you think me so meddlesome?"

She shook her head. "I believe you and your sister are very alike in some ways." She smiled. "Fortunately, I am confident that the decisions you make will be sound ones."

"Are you disappointed I'm not to marry Isabel?"

"No," she said pensively. "The betrothal was thrust upon you against my wishes, when you were a mere ten years old and Isabel a baby. You both should find your own paths in life."

Hugh smiled, pleased that she understood, but his mother was always scrupulously fair. "I'll bring Lucy to see you tomorrow."

"Because her family are not in Society, I know very little about Miss Kershaw. As she's to be my daughter-in-law, I would like to learn more about her. Especially," she said, her eyes twinkling, "as you've been set on her for quite a while."

"Mama. You have been confined to your bedchamber for most of it. How could you know that?"

"Mothers are born with an innate understanding of their children, and I am no different."

"Might it have something to do with Barker, your abigail?"

His mother smiled at him. "A good lady's maid is worth her weight in gold."

"So, you are pleased that Isabel and I didn't marry?" he repeated, needing to be sure, although he would never be swayed from marrying Lucy.

"I wanted you to marry for love, Hugh. And you do love Lucy, don't you?"

"Yes, Mama." He bent to kiss her cheek. "Very much."

He didn't add how impatient he was to make Lucy his wife before he left the room. He had planned to woo Lucy, to arrange the perfect setting to propose, but when he'd seen her, he'd known that none of that had mattered. Only that she would say *yes*.

Chapter Twenty

A S THEY LEFT the church in Piccadilly, which Hugh had suggested would be perfect for the wedding, Lucy turned to him. "The minister was a nice gentleman. "But your mother might wish for something grander. Still, it is such a pretty church. I should love us to be married here. Would it be too small?"

He smiled as he took her arm. "Then we shall have a small wedding." He bent and whispered against her ear, "And the sooner, the better."

Lucy flushed at the promise in his eyes, fearing everyone around them could read their thoughts. But something still nagged at her.

While the Marquess of Berwick's health showed little improvement, it was now an accepted fact that her father stood next in linc for the Kerwick fortune. "What will society make of my declaration that Papa was the heir when he clearly wasn't then? I hope it doesn't impact your family," she said to Hugh when they'd settled in the coach. "Will your mother be upset?"

He smiled down at her his eyes soft. "Mama is delighted we are marrying. I believe my betrothal to Isabel, arranged by my father and Sir Phillip Ashton so many years ago, worried her a good deal. Do not concern yourself, my love. As my countess, you can hold your head up in society and let them think what they will."

Lucy laughed and shook her head.

At the end of the week, Hugh drove to Bath and brought her father back with him. He stayed with Lucy at Aunt Mary's townhouse.

"Life holds many surprises, doesn't it, Lucy?" he said as they sat together in the garden enjoying a hint of summer in the air. He smiled. "I was confident you would find a good man, although I didn't expect someone quite as remarkable as Hugh."

She smiled. "Nor did I, Papa."

The door opened and Aunt Mary emerged carrying Lucy's father's hat. The maid followed with a tray of lemonade. "The sun is quite hot today," Aunt Mary said, handing the hat to Papa.

It amused Lucy how much Aunt Mary bustled around him, seeing to Papa's every comfort. Perhaps she had revised her opinion of him, or was so delighted her niece was to marry an earl that it rendered any criticisms she'd had of him in the past irrelevant. Whatever the reason, Lucy could only be grateful.

If her aunt was disappointed that the wedding was not to be a grand affair held at St. George's, but the small church in Piccadilly, with only close friends and family present, she didn't say so. Lucy appreciated the help she gave her, choosing the white, satin wedding gown and the wisp of white net to dress Lucy's hair, as well as the dowager countess's diamond tiara. Sarah would be Lucy's attendant wearing a white muslin gown. Luke was to be Hugh's best man. Their wedding breakfast would be held at Dorchester House.

Lucy smiled. It was going to be a perfect day, and she would be the wife of the man she loved dearly, something she'd never dreamed was possible.

BEFORE THE ALTAR, with his groomsmen, Luke and Ross, beside him, Hugh watched the lovely young lady in white satin advance down the aisle on her father's arm. A vision, soon to be his wife. His heart turned over. Lucy was beautiful, but also unpredictable. She had been from the moment he first met her, at that ball in Bath where she'd told those two women off. He'd been vastly entertained when moments before he'd been counting the hours until he could decently depart the ball. And then in London, when he'd expected her to flirt and try to sway his opinion, her unprovoked confession about the lie had disarmed him, while her unaffected beauty had entranced him. He desired her with every breath in his body, and God willing, should he spend the next fifty or more years in her company, she would still surprise him, and at times, rob him of breath.

She came to stand beside him, and he gazed into her deep, velvety-brown eyes. "My love," he murmured, after her proud father had placed her in Hugh's care and taken his seat.

Her bridesmaids, Sarah, in white muslin, and a lady in pink, Mrs. Alice Gaskill, Lucy's married friend from Bath who'd come to London to take part in the celebration, joined Luke and Mr. Kershaw in the front pew. Sarah's blue eyes glowed with pleasure, her face less strained and thin, making him aware of how much better she was now that Cardew was gone from her life, and Luke was firmly in it.

Hugh turned to the vicar, who then began the ceremony.

Chapter Twenty-One

THE FEW GUESTS who'd stayed to dinner had finally departed Dorchester House. Hugh's arm around her, Lucy climbed the stairs with him for their first night together. He escorted her in and closed the door to the countess's bedchamber behind him.

"It was a perfect wedding, wasn't it?" Lucy asked, standing on the threshold, observing the elegant splendor which was now to be her bedchamber.

"It was." He drew her close. "Absolutely perfect."

Lucy giggled. "You should have seen Mrs. Vellacott's face when Papa escorted me into the church. She stood outside looking sullen."

Hugh nuzzled her neck. "Who is Mrs. Vellacott?"

Lucy pushed away to gaze up at him, aware that he teased her. "You know full well who she is, Hugh. She's the one who…"

He slid his hand through her hair at the back of her head and pulling gently, raised her face and kissed her. When his tongue pushed at the seam of her lips, Lucy gasped and held on to his coat. She opened for him as a coil of desire stirred low in her belly.

She hung on to him as her knees sagged. His mouth tasted clean, with a hint of champagne.

He released her, and his fingers worked at the buttons on her gown. In a moment, the fabric spooled at her feet along with her petticoat. Her stays soon followed.

In her shift and suddenly shy, she saw the intent in his heavy-lidded blue, blue eyes and quivered. "Do you think that I should…?"

He shook his head with a wry smile. "I have been a patient man, Lucy, but no more."

What she was about to suggest vanished from her mind as he swept her up in his arms and strode across the thick carpet to the enormous four-poster bed draped in gold damask. A gold coverlet was folded over a chair and the sheet pulled back.

He gently laid her down on the satin sheet, then, holding her calf, slipped off her shoe. Stroking up her leg, he pressed a kiss on her thigh and untied her garter. Before she could draw breath, both her stockings were thrown onto a chair. She marveled at his expertise and wondered idly how much experience he'd had with ladies' stockings. Quite a lot, she decided.

Hugh moved away to undress. She watched as he stripped off his clothes. His legs were long and powerful. Tall and lean, he was superbly muscled, his buttocks round and taut, and so different to a woman's body. She curled her fingers with the desire to touch them. He was already aroused and so perfectly male. Her chest tightened, making it hard for her to breathe.

He came back to the bed and stood for a moment, looking down at her. "How beautiful you are, Lucy."

Her breath quickened, and she held up her arms to him. He joined her on the bed. The heat and weight of his body wrapped around her as the rampant sensations he aroused in her demanded more of him. His skin was smooth beneath her questing fingers, the strength and fluid movements of his muscles and tendons beneath fascinating her.

He sat up to remove her shift, and her shyness fled. She lay boldly naked before him.

"Sweetheart." His voice guttural, his rough palm closed over her breast, and he thumbed a nipple until she whimpered. His warm breath feathered across her skin as his finger circled the sensitive, puckered nub.

When he drew the other nipple into his mouth, an aching tension throbbed between her legs. Lucy clutched his hair and moaned softly. She murmured his name, begging him, wanting him to ease the pleasure-pain that built low down in her stomach.

As Lucy's hands stroked over his arms and shoulders, Hugh's loins throbbed. He'd wanted this for too long. He was conscious of this being Lucy's first time and didn't want to hurt her. After all, they had all the time in the world. His fingers stroked the hard nub within her soft folds, feeling the slick moisture, evidence of her desire, while she murmured incoherently. Then he moved between her legs and settled himself against her.

Lucy grew still.

"It will be all right in a moment," he said as he pushed a little way. Then he waited for her body to accept him. He moved again, and an explosion of heat enveloped him, threatening to draw him in farther like a siren's call. He clamped his teeth and moved slowly, watching Lucy's face. Her tongue traced her swollen lips, her hands gripping his shoulders so tightly, her nails dug into his skin.

Hugh kissed her deeply and increased his pace. She moaned against his lips, pushing up her hips to meet him.

Wrapping his arms under her bottom to raise her higher, he thrust harder. When Lucy's body tightened around him, he gave in to his release. His body shuddered and with a deep cry, he fell back.

Hugh moved to her side and raised himself on an elbow. "Did it hurt, sweetheart?"

She shook her head, her eyelids half-closed. "It was lovely."

He kissed her, then drew the sheet and blanket over them. "I love you. Sleep, my love."

"I love you, Hugh," she murmured as she closed her eyes.

Hugh lay beside her, his thoughts drifting. He'd never believed in this kind of love before. He'd known deep down in his soul for some time that Lucy was the one. He smiled. She was his at last.

Epilogue

Three Months Later

T HE COACH TRUNDLED north. Lucy opened her eyes and raised her head from Hugh's chest, where she'd slumbered. "Where are we now?"

"A little farther advanced from the last time you asked me," Hugh said with a grin.

"Oh, you." She laughed and sat up to peer through the window at the passing scene. There was nothing remarkable to see, merely trees and a farmer in the fields.

"It's a long journey to Carlisle," Hugh said. "We are about halfway. We'll reach the inn in less than an hour, where we'll dine and spend the night."

"Good." Lucy thought their nights spent at inns were the best part of the journey. She gazed at her handsome husband speculatively.

He raised his eyebrows. "What goes on in your pretty head, my love?"

"Must we leave early in the morning again?" She loved their mornings lying sleepy and warm beside him.

"If we intend to reach the Berwick estate within a fortnight," he said, tracing a finger along her bottom lip.

She nodded with some regret. "Papa is expecting us. I don't

wish him to worry."

He smiled. "No, of course not, sweetheart."

"Sarah and Luke's wedding was delightful, wasn't it? Sarah made a lovely bride."

"They'll be back from Brighton when we return and shall come to stay with us at Woodcroft."

She sighed. "So much has happened since our wedding. Aunt Mary writing from Ireland. She seems so happy to have found Anabel content and well cared for. Although she expressed some shock that they are not yet married. But it will take some time for the divorce to go through, I imagine."

"Mm," Hugh said, picking up the newspaper he'd purchased at their last stop.

"And that letter from Mrs. Benton," Lucy said to distract him from reading. "So good to learn she has safely given birth to a daughter, Hannah. I do hope she will write again. I'd like to know more about that exotic country." She smiled. "I should like to visit her."

"Certainly not!" he glanced at her. "Are you teasing me, my lady? I don't believe that for a moment."

Hugh shoved away the newspaper. He put his arms around her and, lowering his head to hers, kissed her long and deeply.

Lucy gasped. She reached up to push back a lock of his dark hair, which had fallen over his forehead. "Are you trying to distract me, my lord?"

"That is my intention," he said, pulling her onto his lap. "It's time we christened the carriage."

"Oh, no! Hugh!"

"Surely, an improper lady, such as yourself, traveling about with a gentleman without a chaperone, and staying at inns, while failing to always be completely truthful, wouldn't say *no*?"

Lucy giggled. "Please do put down the blinds! Or the *ton* shall believe me to be even more improper."

About the Author

A USA TODAY bestselling author of Regency romances, with over 35 books published, Maggi's Regency series are International bestsellers. Stay tuned for Maggi's latest Regency series out next year. Her novels include Victorian mysteries, contemporary romantic suspense and young adult. Maggi holds a BA in English and Master of Arts Degree in Creative Writing. She supports the RSPCA and animals often feature in her books.

Like to keep abreast of my latest news? Join my newsletter.
http://bit.ly/1m70lJJ

Blog: http://bit.ly/1t7B5dx
Find excerpts and reviews on my website: http://bit.ly/1m70lJJ
Twitter: @maggiandersen: http://bit.ly/1Aq8eHg
Facebook: Maggi Andersen Author: http://on.fb.me/1KiyP9g
Goodreads: http://bit.ly/1TApe0A
Pinterest: https://www.pinterest.com.au/maggiandersen

Maggi's Amazon page for her books with Dragonblade Publishing.
https://tinyurl.com/y34dmquj